Quiet Places, Warm Thoughts

A Collection
of
Stories & Poems

by
Janette Oke

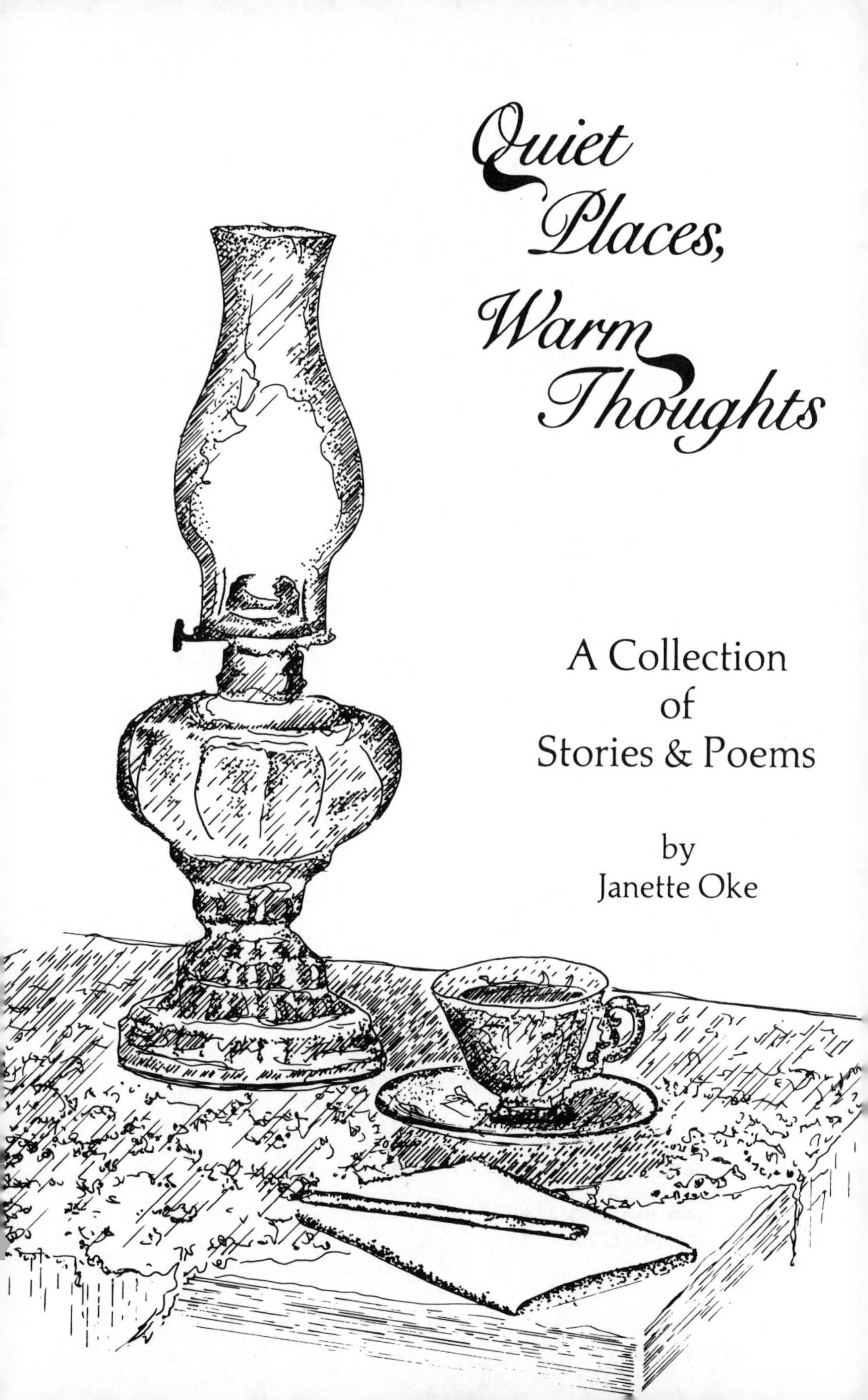
Quiet Places, Warm Thoughts
A Collection of Stories & Poems
by Janette Oke

by Bethel Publishing, Elkhart, IN 46516

ISBN 0-934998-15-9
Printed in U.S.A.

To my dear and only brother,
John Frederick (Jack) Steeves.

He taught me many things —
how to take teasing without getting mad —
how to drive his stick-shift car uphill —
how to chase muskrats in spring-swollen ditches —
and how to accept handouts gratefully
when I was a "poverty-stricken college student."

He also provided me with a super-special
sister-in-law, Ila Strand Steeves.

I love them both, along with their
"original five" plus additions.

Table of Contents

The Storm 9
The Love That Gave 30
Insight 33
A Matter of Trust 35
Son 46
Mommy, You Come with Me 48
A Son Is Born 50
The Easter Story 52
Emmaus 57
An Apple for the Teacher 60
Sin in the Camp 67
I Wish I Was a Turtle 76
No Strings Attached 82
Mother's Apron Strings 85
They Just Have Everything 89
A Lesson from Sandra 97
Discard 103

The Storm

Marcia Lambert could feel the cold fear gripping her, freezing the beating of her heart as she watched the windshield wipers doggedly trying to keep the windshield clear of the driving snow.

Frantically, she glanced sideways at the two little snow-suited forms in the car seats beside her. They were both asleep, unaware of the danger surrounding them.

The car was slowing down as the huge drifts piled higher, pulling slightly off course when it was forced to take the larger drifts.

"Please, please . . ." Marcia urged it on.

If only she had checked the forecast before leaving home.

She fought the car on, straining ahead to see the road through the thick porridge of snow. Then, with a thump, the car shuddered and stopped. She knew that she was stuck—miles from nowhere and in a raging blizzard. Her attempts to coax it, either forward or back, met with failure.

Her fear was not for herself but for the babies beside her. For a moment panic seized her. She wanted to grab them up and run through the storm. She forced herself to sit still and think before making a move. With a sob she pressed her forehead to the steering wheel and began to pray.

"Oh, God," she pleaded, "please send someone to us. Don't let the babies die out here."

She continued praying and pleading for some minutes. The storm seemed even more fierce when she raised her head.

She wiped her tears with the corner of her scarf.

One of the little ones stirred. She reached in the back for a blanket to cover him, then began taking note.

The time was six forty-five. She had expected to be home by nine-thirty, but because of the storm she was probably behind her schedule by almost an hour. The gas would last for about two hours—with luck. Even with the motor running, the car was cooling off in the sub-zero weather. When the gas was gone . . . she didn't want to think about it.

She scratched at the window in vain, trying to clean a spot to see out. There was nothing but snow to see anyway, swirling and mocking—seeming to gloat over the fact that it was the victor.

The minutes ticked by slowly; the car was getting cooler. She reached for another blanket to cover the other baby. Again she prayed. It was getting very dark.

Donnie stirred again, then began to cry. She tried to hush him, but it was far past his supper hour and now he was cold as well.

He cried harder, and as Marcia had expected, Donna awoke to accompany him. Marcia cuddled them close and rocked gently, wishing with all her heart that she too could cry.

She blinked. Was that a light? Somewhere through the storm she had thought that she'd seen a dim spark of light.

"Oh, God," she prayed, "please help us."

In a moment the snow seemed to slacken somewhat and again Marcia saw the light. She also saw in thankfulness, as though a miracle hand had suddenly placed it there, the outline of a building. Quickly she bundled both babies close and pushed hard against the door. For a moment it refused to budge, then slowly she felt it give against the drifted snow outside. In sudden afterthought Marcia turned and switched off the key. She had almost left the car running.

Half running, half stumbling, she headed for the light. If only she could make it before the storm blocked it from view.

A few more yards to go, she prodded herself. A sudden gust of wind whipped snow into her face. She could see nothing.

"Keep going straight ahead—straight."

She stumbled on.

"Oh, God. Help me not to miss it."

The cabin's darkness loomed right before her. In the blinding snow, she had almost walked into it. She felt along the wall for the door and thumped it with her foot. She didn't have to wait long until it opened and she felt the warmth of the room strike her face.

For a moment she felt herself reeling; someone was helping her inside, taking the crying twins from her arms. He placed a chair for her and she sank down on it.

"I'm stuck," she said, in answer to the question she could feel.

"You carried both of these through this storm?"

He indicated the rather pudgy snowsuit-clad twins.

She managed a weak smile.

"I could have carried four—if they'd been mine and out there."

"Yes, I guess so."

He turned and called softly.

"Mother."

A woman entered the room, carrying a kerosene lamp. Her hair was greying but she looked young for her years, except somehow for her eyes. There was a certain oldness in her eyes. Marcia couldn't judge what it was—fear, anger, pain—she couldn't tell.

At the sight of Marcia, the woman stopped, then whirled and stared at Donnie who had started to cry again. The strange look in her eyes deepened. Donna squirmed and the woman swung around to her.

"Not two of them."

She turned to her son and demanded almost angrily, "What are you going to do?"

"Only one thing to do," he responded pleasantly enough. "I'll unbundle them and you get them something to eat."

"And after that?"

"The storm will decide for us. They can't go out in it while it's like this."

Marcia stood awkward and helpless. The man began to unbundle the babies; the woman, still bristling, turned to the stove to heat some soup and fix some tea.

"You were lucky to find us," the man said. "This is the only cabin for eleven miles to the east and fifteen to the west."

Marcia blinked, then slowly smiled.

"It wasn't luck," she said evenly. "It was God."

She thought he showed surprise at first; then with a nod he returned to unbundling Donna.

The roaring fire felt good to Marcia. She had received quite a chill in coming the short distance to the cabin.

Doug Morgan was the man at the cabin. He was the forest ranger for the area—miles and miles of timber and foothills.

His mother, Mrs. Ruth Morgan, had moved in with him five months earlier, and from what Marcia seemed to observe, something was amiss. [She didn't seem to be there just because of concern for the well-being of her son.]

Finally, the twins had been fed and put to bed, one on each end of the cot. They slept peacefully, paying no heed to the howling storm outside.

Earlier in the evening, Doug Morgan had bundled up, tied one end of a long rope to himself and the other to the rail on the cabin steps, and made two trips to the car to bring in the luggage. The car, it turned out, was only a couple hundred feet from the cabin; even so, at times the snow would shut out completely the dim light from the cabin. As Marcia realized how close she had been to the cabin when she became stuck in the drift and the many miles in either direction without any resident, she bowed her head in deep thankfulness. Surely God's hand was in this and yet . . . .

The agitation in the cabin seemed to intensify. Marcia was troubled by it. How long would they be here? she wondered. She cast a glance at Mrs. Morgan and hoped it would not be long.

"How old are the twins?"

Marcia jumped at the sound of Doug's voice.

"Oh, sorry." She attempted a laugh. "I was deep in thought. They just had their first birthday last week."

"Quite a pair," was his only comment.

"If I might ask," said Mrs. Morgan coolly, "what are you doing way out here on a night like this?"

Marcia laughed again, in an effort to thaw out this woman.

"It is silly, isn't it? I was going home for Christmas. My folks haven't seen the twins since they were just tiny. I was going to surprise them. They live at North Fork."

"North Fork! That's a hundred and forty-eight miles from here," commented Doug.

"Didn't you hear the storm warning?" Mrs. Morgan scowled.

Marcia smiled and waved a hand casually.

"Do you know," she said, "I never even thought to turn the radio on . . . I was so excited about going home."

The older woman frowned, and the smile left Marcia's face. Switch back to the babies, Marcia told herself. She nodded at them.

"They're sleeping like there wasn't any storm. They sure were getting hungry though."

"What is it you call them?" Doug asked.

Mrs. Morgan seemed not to hear.

"Donna and Donald. My husband named our unborn baby Donald. He said every firstborn should be a boy. When Donna arrived too, I couldn't think of any other name for her."

Marcia laughed again.

"My husband was so excited about being a father that it's a wonder he came up with *any* name."

"Suppose he's real proud—"

"He's never seen them," Marcia cut in. The expression on her face didn't change, but her eyes did. She hurried on.

"My husband was killed in a hunting accident six months before the babies were born."

She saw the look of sympathy on Doug's face and noticed that Mrs. Morgan suddenly seemed to come alive too. Giving neither a chance to speak, she continued.

"Tom would have been very proud of his babies. Donna looks just like him, and Donnie's eyes twinkle like his—though help us if he has his father's teasing ability."

She laughed.

"He already—"

Mrs. Morgan rose, her face a picture of distaste.

"It seems to me that, with the death of your husband such a short time ago, you couldn't have cared much—the way you chat and laugh and carry on."

Marcia gasped; the color drained from her face. She rose from her chair and looked straight into the angry grey eyes. Finally her voice and composure returned.

"Mrs. Morgan," she said evenly, "any of us may face tragedy in life. When we do, it's up to us how we are going to meet it and react to it. Until—"

But the older woman wheeled away and was gone.

Marcia stood trembling for awhile and then turned to the fire to try to thaw the chill from her heart with the heat of the blaze.

Some minutes passed, and finally Doug spoke.

"Don't be too hard on Mother," he said softly. "She has had a pretty deep hurt and the wound is still fresh and pains a lot."

He hesitated for a moment, then went on.

"Almost a year ago my only sister died in childbirth. The baby, little Robert, lived. Since then, Mother has locked herself away from life. She thinks that she hates little Robbie for taking Janie away. Oh, I know. It's foolish. But Mother is all mixed up in her pain. Seeing these babies has only reopened the wound.

"To make matters worse, we got a letter from Bob, my brother-in-law, just a couple of days ago. He has done everything he can to keep Robbie with him, but now the housekeeper that he had is in the hospital with cancer and he can't find another. He's afraid that Robbie will have to be placed in a home until he is able to make some kind of arrangements. The poor man is worried sick.

"Mother hasn't said anything, but I know that she is

having quite a battle."

Marcia sat wide-eyed. All that she could manage was an "Oh-h."

How could a woman be so cruel? To blame an innocent little baby for the death of the mother, then stand back and let welfare take it from the father who had already lost so much. What kind of a person was this Mrs. Morgan anyway?

Suddenly Marcia arose.

"I think I'll get some sleep," she said, her voice a little shaky.

She looked at the sleeping babies. Doug's eyes followed hers.

"Don't worry about them," he said. "I'm going to stay up most of the night to mind the fire. I'll see that they're okay."

"Thank you," she murmured and was gone.

Once in bed, Marcia's head seemed to whirl. Mrs. Morgan's words kept ringing in her ears—"couldn't have cared much . . . chat and laugh and carry on." How could she know how much of her had died with her Tom? Only the thought of her coming baby had kept her world together. At times even that didn't seem enough to keep fighting for. How could Mrs. Morgan know that the laughter and chatter were a cover-up for the hurt beneath? How could she know of Marcia's little game of pretend?

In all of the months since Tom's death, Marcia had never let herself really face the truth. She kept going on pretending. Oh, yes, she could say the words—Tom is dead—but she never let herself believe them.

What had she told Mrs. Morgan? We all may face tragedy—it's up to us how we are going to meet it. Marcia saw clearly now that she hadn't chosen the right way.

Life was no game of pretend.

"He's not coming back," she told herself. "He's not

coming back."

The words began to sink in.

"Oh, Tom, Tom," she sobbed into her pillow. "You're gone—for always—and I miss you so much."

Mrs. Morgan prepared for bed in anger. She didn't know if the anger that she felt was toward Marcia or herself. What could Marcia know of sorrow? But then, hadn't Marcia faced it too? How could she act so glib, so matter-of-fact, so light about it?

"I hate these Pollyannas," Mrs. Morgan fumed, but her thoughts returned to Bob.

He had loved Janie too. Yet, somehow, he also loved the small baby that took Janie's life. Mrs. Morgan puzzled over that. It made her angry with her son-in-law. Maybe he hadn't loved Janie as much as he had pretended to.

So what if the little mite did go to a home? Probably the best thing anyway. Besides Bob would likely marry some good-for-nothing young thing and Robbie would only be in the way.

Still in anger, Mrs. Morgan put out her light and crawled into bed. She pulled the covers close.

"That mournful, hateful blizzard," she thought. "Why did it have to bring that unwanted woman and her two babies here anyway?"

With a troubled spirit, Mrs. Morgan tried to get some sleep.

Doug Morgan reached for another log for the fire. What a night! Mentally he reviewed it. Too bad that Mother was so upset by the visitors. It would only worsen things for poor Bob. Why did all of this happen to a guy as nice as Bob? But then—life seemed to withhold no punches from anyone just because they were good. Take this Marcia; she seemed like such a nice young woman to have been through so much. Now this. Certainly this wasn't a very happy situation to find oneself in . . . stuck in a howling blizzard with a thirty-year-old, rather sour bachelor and his bitter, widowed mother who deeply resented the presence of the babies.

"Hope this storm doesn't last long," he muttered; but, as he crossed to look down on the sleeping babies, he wasn't sure if that were altogether true. A loneliness that he hadn't been aware of seemed to make his whole body ache.

He began to wonder if he hadn't missed a lot in life. The seven years of living alone out at the ranger station, his boasting to many that this was the life that he was cut out for—was it as true as he pretended it to be?

He shook the thoughts from him and returned to the fire. Of course he was happy out here. It was just this crazy storm. He hoped it didn't last too long.

Marcia's first thought as she awakened the next morning was the one she had gone to sleep with the night before . . . he's not coming back. Strangely enough, it didn't hurt as deeply as it had the night before. She missed Tom terribly—she supposed that she always would—but there was a peace which had come to her. She wouldn't have to clown anymore. She could be a real person again. She wasn't aware of it, but somehow a new gentleness was hers because of her experience. She seemed closer to God too—perhaps because she realized, now that she had faced reality, that she needed Him even more.

Then she remembered Mrs. Morgan. Poor thing, she thought. She must be hurt awfully deep to be reacting in this way.

Marcia decided to look up Bob Lawton when she got to Bent River to tell him that she would gladly keep little Robbie until he could find someone to care for him. The poor father. She knew how she'd feel if someone were to take her precious babies from her.

Her babies! She suddenly sat bolt upright and listened hard. No crying. Then she heard Donna's merry giggle and Doug saying softly, "This is the way the ladies ride."

Mrs. Morgan said something in return and though Marcia couldn't hear the words, she could catch the tone—still one of disgust and anger at being stuck with these unwelcome guests.

Marcia went to the window, hoping to see improvement in the weather, but was disappointed when she drew back the curtain. The storm raged on. Reluctantly, she dressed and went out. She was greeted by squeals of delight from her two small babies. Donnie ran to meet her and received a big hug. Donna was unwilling to leave her ride but finally crawled off and toddled over, lest Donnie get all of the loving.

Marcia smiled her good morning to Doug, then turned to Mrs. Morgan.

"Good morning," she said. "May I help you with breakfast?"

She noted that Mrs. Morgan appeared older this morning. Perhaps it was just that she hadn't slept well. Her attitude had not changed.

"Just take care of your babies," she almost snapped. "Seems to me that that's a big enough job for two or three people."

Marcia felt the sting of the words. Had they been misbehaving? She hadn't heard anything. She said a little prayer, then prepared the cereal for the twins. When it was time to feed them, Doug took up one dish and began to feed Donnie who was pounding the table impatiently.

Marcia sighed in relief. She was afraid that the demanding baby would anger Mrs. Morgan even more.

After the twins had been fed, they were put on the floor to play while the others had their breakfast. Marcia noticed Doug watching them with interest but said nothing.

Mrs. Morgan must have noticed too, for as the minutes ticked by, she seemed to become even more antagonistic.

She scowled at the day; she scolded Doug for the poor firewood; she fretted about Prince, Doug's German shepherd, who was scratching at the garage door and howling to be set free. Marcia felt that none of these things was the real reason for Mrs. Morgan's present mood.

The older woman tried to ignore the twins, but no one could miss their chatter and squeals as they rolled tins of soup and pork 'n beans back and forth across the floor. Suddenly Donna picked up a tin and saw the Campbell's soup kid on the label.

"Oh," she said, smiling at it. She toddled to Mrs. Morgan and leaned against her knee, holding up the can.

"Ba-by," she cooed.

For a minute Mrs. Morgan's eyes seemed to soften; then she reached down and rather roughly pushed Donna away.

Quickly Doug pushed back from the table and swept Donna into his arms. He walked away to the window.

"A baby, eh," he said.

Donna's smile returned.

"Ba-by," she said, holding out the can for him to see.

Mrs. Morgan went to the stove in the pretense of getting another cup of coffee. Marcia noted when the table was cleared that the cup had not been touched.

Marcia stood at the window, watching the storm rage on. She wondered where the storm was the most intense, inside or outside of the cabin walls.

Mrs. Morgan had prepared dinner, then had gone to

her room—she couldn't stand the noise, she had snapped as she left.

True, it had been noisy, Marcie had to admit. Against his Mother's wishes, Doug had brought Prince into the cabin. The temperature made even the garage too cold for the dog. Donna and Donnie had squealed with delight at the sight of the dog, and to everyone's surprise he seemed to like them just as much as they liked him. They rolled and romped and played—certainly it was noisy, Marcia acknowledged.

When Mrs. Morgan left the room, Doug's face showed some concern. He turned to the fire for a moment, silent in thought. Marcia bit her lip. She wanted to cry. When she felt that she had control of herself, she crossed to Doug.

"I'm terribly sorry that we've upset everything so. If only—"

"Nonsense," he interrupted. "This is a battle that Mother's just going to have to fight out alone."

He shook his head and smiled.

"Well, let's have dinner."

He picked up Donna who was sitting half on Prince and half on the rug.

"Want some dinner, Princess?"

Marcia blinked back the tears. How glad she was that he seemed to like the babies rather than resent them as his mother did. She hoped that she wouldn't have to impose upon him for long. She cast a glance at the window but could see only the white whirling snow driven by an angry wind.

Mrs. Morgan stayed in her room for the remainder of the day. Marcia took over the kitchen, getting the meal and doing the dishes with Doug's help. The twins were put to bed early, and after briefly trying to read, Marcia excused herself and went to bed also.

Doug sat alone before the fire, pretending to read *Field and Stream,* but his thoughts were far from the story of the hunters in a remote mountain area.

Instead of envying them in their aloneness as he had so often done in the past, he felt strangely uneasy. He almost shivered at the thought.

"Face it," he finally said to himself. "You are about the loneliest man alive, and you've only yourself to thank for it."

He tossed aside the magazine and began to pace in front of the fire.

Before his eyes seemed to flash again the picture of a pretty face. It was a beautiful face—he had always thought so. Carma Williams was the name that it bore. It seemed to Doug that he had always loved Carma, but of course that wasn't quite true, for he had been nineteen before he had even met her.

For some reason, this beautiful girl who moved to his town with her hotel-managing father, had chosen Doug from among all of her many admirers. Doug had felt ten feet tall.

He wanted to shower her with all of the good things in life, but as yet he could afford none of them.

Carma's voice, her eyes, her long dark hair, seemed to capture his every thought, yet all of the time that he loved her, he knew that it wasn't right.

"Be ye not unequally yoked together."

Doug was a Christian; Carma an unbeliever.

He tried to shrug it off when she made cutting remarks about his faith. She doesn't understand yet, he'd tell himself. But inwardly he knew that, as the weeks went by, he was getting further away from God instead of Carma being drawn to Him.

One night, after a particularly trying Sunday at the beach with Carma, God seemed to pin Doug down.

"It's either her or me," God seemed to say.

"But I can't give her up," Doug sobbed into his pillow. "I can't. I can't." Still he clung to God too, seeming to bargain for time, hoping that time would somehow resolve the problem.

The next morning he heard the news: sometime in the night hours, Carma had eloped with the bartender from her Dad's hotel.

Doug was stunned. He couldn't go to work that day. Somehow he felt that God had maliciously taken away this one whom he loved.

He hated life; he hated women. For awhile he thought that he hated Carma, but he wasn't sure.

His only desire was to get away from everyone and everything, off by himself, so he packed up and left town. He drove to the city and signed up for the life of a forest ranger, relieved at the thought of being away from fickle people.

As he unpacked his few possessions, Carma's picture was among them. Through the months and even years, that smiling, teasing face became his little shrine. It was a symbol to him of what life—or God—had cost him.

All of these years he had felt as one of God's martyrs who had been asked to give up all for his faith. Doug had even come to the place where he mouthed the words, "Thy will be done." Still, he kept the picture as a reminder of the price that he had paid.

Tonight, as Doug paced before the open fire, then turned to look at the sleeping babies, he began to see things differently.

Suddenly he whirled and went to a chest in the corner of the room. He removed a picture and returned to the fire. For a moment he stood looking at it. For the first time he saw the face as it really was. Though young—and, yes, pretty—sin had already given it a hardened look. The chin held a stubbornness that Doug had never noticed before; and the smiling, yet mocking, eyes seemed to have a coldness that almost made Doug shiver.

"What a fool I've been, Lord," he muttered. "What a senseless fool. To think that I thought that you were denying me love and a home. With her, life would have held nothing but misery and heartache. Forgive me, God—forgive me."

He tore the picture in two and tossed it into the fire.

"Thank you, Lord. Thank you for sparing me a life like that."

A verse of scripture ran through his mind.

"All things work together for good . . . ."

"All things—even though we don't see it at the time. You haven't withheld love and a home from me—you've preserved me for it. Someday—"

Doug's thoughts were interrupted by a cry from Donnie. He crossed to the baby, who held up his arms to be picked up. Gently, Doug lifted him and pulled the rocker closer to the fire. He felt at peace with life and with God as he cuddled Donnie close and began to rock.

Marcia noticed a difference in Doug the next morning, but she couldn't decide just what it was. Perhaps it was relief that the storm seemed to be slackening, she told herself.

Mrs. Morgan was around again, but she seemed even more at odds with life than before. Doug didn't even seem to notice, as he cheerfully entertained the two small guests and chatted amicably with Marcia.

In mid-afternoon the storm subsided. Marcia was much relieved, but as she looked out at the mountainous drifts, she realized that it would be some time yet before the plows would be through so that she could once again be on her way.

Her car was almost buried, and looking at its closeness to the cabin made Marcia thankful again for the miracle that had caused her to get stuck so near to help.

How thankful she was that her folks hadn't known of her plans. They would have been worried sick had they known that she started out shortly before the storm.

"Well," she tried to cheer herself, "it shouldn't be long now."

Of course it would take a bit of extra time to look up Bob Lawton in Bent River to see what could be done for Robbie. The thought of caring for three one-year-olds was a bit staggering, but Marcia assured herself that somehow God would help her to cope. Maybe it wouldn't be for too long.

Marcia turned from the window to see Doug pulling on his heavy jacket.

"Now that the storm's over," he said, "I can replenish the wood supply. It was getting dangerously low."

"Let me help you," Marcia quickly responded. "It would do me good to get out."

Mrs. Morgan cast a fearful glance at the two sleeping babies. Marcia followed her thoughts but said nothing. To her surprise Doug said it for her.

"They'll be okay."

Marcia bundled up and together she and Doug fought their way through the high drifts toward the wood supply.

Prince bounded through the snow, thankful for a chance to be outside again.

Mrs. Morgan watched them go, then turned back to her knitting, now and than casting an apprehensive look in the direction of the babies.

The fire began to die down, so she laid aside the half-knit mitten and went for another log. In carrying it to the fire, she tripped over the corner of the rug, and the log fell to the floor with a loud crash.

Both babies jumped but only Donnie awakened. The noise startled him and he began to cry.

Without a second thought Mrs. Morgan reached down and picked him up. As the soft baby arms encircled her neck she suddenly thought of her own little Robbie—her Janie's precious baby.

Loneliness for her only daughter seeped through her, and along with it a strange longing to hold the grandchild that she had never seen.

"Oh, God," she whispered as tears began to stream down her face.

She buried her head against the small baby that she held close and sobbed out all of the pent-up bitterness. How disappointed Janie would be at her feeling toward Robbie; how ashamed Mrs. Morgan felt for so ridiculously holding Janie's death against the tiny baby.

"Oh, God, forgive me—forgive me. I've been so blind in my sorrow—so foolish."

When she finally lifted her tear-stained face, the eyes were soft with love. She looked younger than she had for many months.

She smiled at Donnie who looked at her almost fearfully; then his tiny face responded with a smile, and he reached his hand up to touch a tear on her cheek.

She laughed at this and pulled him close again.

She rocked him in her arms, gently back and forth, and when she looked down again, it was at a sleeping baby. Gently she laid him down and went to the kitchen to do some special baking.

When Marcia and Doug returned with a hand sleigh loaded high with firewood, the first thing to greet them was the smell of hot muffins.

"Oh," Marcia said, "I hadn't realized how hungry I am."

She blinked. Did Mrs. Morgan smile? Marcia had never seen the woman smile. Doug had noticed it too. Marcia could tell by the look on his face, but neither of them made comment.

"Thought we'd have some afternoon tea," Mrs. Morgan explained.

The table was all ready, and soon the three of them were sitting enjoying tea and hot muffins with honey.

In an effort to be very casual, Mrs. Morgan began.

"I was wondering, Marcia, if you'd have room for me to ride with you as far as Bent River?"

She noted the shocked looks on the faces before her.

"I mean—well—Bob needs me worse than Doug does—that is—well—you know . . . ."

She couldn't continue. A tear trickled down her cheek.

"Well," she finished lamely, "can't a woman have a change of heart?"

The tears began to flow. Marcia brushed some away from her own eyes.

"Mother," Doug said, taking her hand, "I think that's wonderful."

Marcia's tears were coming too fast to lightly brush away now.

"Thank you, God," she whispered.

Little Robbie was to have someone who cared.

The next morning Marcia awakened to the sound of the snowplow. She jumped out of bed and rushed to the window. There it was—pushing back the drifted snow. Soon she could be on her way again.

Her mind began to leap ahead to what must be done before she'd be ready to go.

Only two days until Christmas. She'd still make it home easily—and with a day to spare.

When she reached the large living room, she found that Mrs. Morgan's suitcases were already packed and at the door. Again, she marveled at the change in this woman. It was going to be a pleasure, and a help, to have her company to Bent River.

Mrs. Morgan was bustling about preparing a lunch for them to take along, giving special thought to what would be the most suitable for the twins.

Marcia felt happy enough to burst, and then she looked at Doug's face. She wasn't prepared for what she saw there. He felt her looking at him and quickly responded with a smile.

Marcia felt sorry for him. Of course he would miss his mother. How selfish she had been not to think of him. He had been most thoughtful of her and had been so good to the twins.

She tried to push the look in his eyes from her thoughts, but somehow it remained to trouble her. If only she could help him in some way. He deserved to be happy. He was one of the nicest people that she had ever met.

Automatically, Marcia went about the things that must be done in order to prepare for leaving.

Doug went out and cleared the remaining snow away from her car and started it for her so that it would be warm for them.

Finally, things were packed and in the car, and they were ready to put on their coats. Doug helped bundle the twins and Marcia didn't think to question it.

At long last, they were all in the car ready to go. Marcia noticed again the lonely look in Doug's eyes.

Suddenly, she realized that it was at her car door he stood, rather than at his mother's. His glance kept going to the babies who reached out to him. Donna patted the seat beside her, wanting him to come too.

Doug smiled, but Marcia felt that it was a rather weak one.

"I can't thank you enough for all that you've done for us," Marcia said sincerely.

"It's been my pleasure," he responded.

Marcia looked at him. For a moment their eyes met and held. Marcia found herself speaking.

"Look," she said, "could you drive over to my folks' for Christmas Day? We'd all love to have you. Just ask anyone in town for Dave Smith. The twins—" She didn't have to finish, for already he was answering.

"I'd love to. I'll really miss the little rascals."

She smiled at him and he smiled back. The lonely look was gone from his eyes.

He stepped back and with a wave she moved the car forward and was once again on her way.

The Love That Gave

Pastor Robinson pushed back from his desk and walked to his study window. A feathery snowfall was cleaning up the world outside, but the pastor scarcely noticed. His thoughts were with his congregation. For three years now he had been their pastor—had preached and prayed and given all that he had. He knew that there were needs among his people, but somehow he couldn't seem to reach them.

"If only they could understand how much God loves them," he thought. "God's love—that's it. On Sunday I'll preach on John 3:16—'The Love That Gave.' "

All week long the pastor worked on his sermon—studying, praying, wording, and rewording.

"Please, dear Lord," he prayed, "may there be a breakthrough. May souls be saved."

Christmas Sunday came. Again the snow was falling. The pastor stood in the foyer, greeting those who came; but even as he smiled and spoke, his heart was heavy with thoughts of his sermon.

"If only I had an illustration of love that they could understand, to capture their attention—something that would make them think."

It was then that he saw the Smiths—a young couple with their two adopted children. He watched as they unbundled the baby and hung up the little boy's coat. He thought as he watched—if ever I have seen a living illustration of love, there it is.

Little Kathy Smith was six months old, and today Susan Smith had her looking like a living Christmas doll in her frilly red and white dress and dainty patent leather shoes with tiny bows. In her short, soft hair was placed a little red ribbon. Yes, here was love.

Suddenly, the minister crossed to Susan Smith and spoke a few words. Would she mind if he used little Kathy as a sermon illustration? He then would have one of the ushers return her to the nursery.

She smiled in agreement and went to join her husband and young son.

The service proceeded as usual, and after the choir's number, Pastor Robinson took his place.

"I've something to show you," he said, moving to the door that led off the platform. He returned with the tiny, smiling baby dressed in her red and white frills.

"Did any of you ever see 'love' before? Well, here it is—from the red bow in her curly hair to the sole of the little red shoe."

Down in the congregation the eyes of a little five-year-old boy lit up at the sight of his baby sister. He smiled, his full attention taken. Love was there—but nobody noticed. All eyes were on the baby, and the response that only a baby can demand held each one. The minister sensed it. He smiled.

"How would you like to find this precious bundle under your tree Christmas morning? Or, better still, how would you like to take her home with you now? If I were to say I'd give—"

"No."

Suddenly all attention was turned from the minister to a small boy who ran down the aisle. He climbed the steps to the platform and stood before the minister, his eyes filled with fear.

"No," he repeated. He swallowed hard. "If you have to give someone away, take me. *She* needs Mommy and Daddy. Please," he pleaded, as the tears began to fill his eyes and his chin trembled in spite of his fight to control it. "She's my little sister and I love her."

"She's my little sister and I love her."

He reached up and grabbed the two pudgy, kicking legs and burying his face against them began to sob.

In the congregation a mother and father looked at one another in shock, then she leaned her head against him and began to weep.

Heads began to bow and people began to cry. The minister stood transfixed. He hadn't meant to frighten the small boy. Tears were running down his own cheeks. An usher stepped forward to take the baby, her brother still clinging to her, back to her parents.

The pastor finally got control enough to step to his pulpit and say in a trembling voice, "Oh, if only you knew how much God loves you."

Slowly Mr. McArthur, an elderly man for whom the church had prayed for years, made his way tearfully to the altar. Next came Beth Boyd, a wayward teenager who had sent her mother to bed in tears and agony of heart many a night. Others followed—Christians came to pray and God's Holy Spirit moved among the people.

In the back of the church a little boy wiped away his tears and smiled at his baby sister, and she reached down to pat-a-cake on his cheek with a soft baby hand. Yes, love was there—the whole church felt it—"The Love That Gave."

Insight

"Hey, Mom . . . C'mon. I've got something to show ya."

He came in with excitement in his voice and feet.

"We've got a flower."

"Oh, really? Where?"

"Out there by the fence—by the rose bush. Come see."

"Will I need my boots?" I asked, turning from the sink and drying my hands.

"Yeah."

He went to get them for me, talking as he went.

"It's still slishy-slushy, an' there's puddles and baby snow drifts. Know what? The snow drifts are getting littler an' littler an' the puddles are getting fatter."

He placed my boots for me.

"You'd better wear your coat, too—it's kinda chillish."

The back closet door clicked as he went for my coat. He had to jump to get it, but made it on the second try. The hanger came down, too, clattering on the floor.

"That's all right," he said. "I'll pick it up when we get back."

He held my coat for me, even though he was too small to reach my shoulders; then he took my hand and we went out and down the steps together.

"We'll have to cross this big puddle. Isn't it getting

big? Don't get your boots full."

He had heard that often enough. He enjoyed sloshing through puddles.

"Here it is."

We knelt together.

"It's blue—not blue like your new dress with the funny buttons but sorta like—no, not like my tuggy tug-boat—more like—more like the mitts Grandma made me. 'Member? Blue like that."

I reached down and touched the soft petals.

"It's not all born yet."

I smiled, knowing what he meant, visualizing the feathers of a chick slowly coming free from the shell.

"It's beautiful. It's a crocus. And look," I said, feeling out each one, "the warm sunshine is going to give it brothers and sisters—here and here and here."

"Really?" his voice shone. "Isn't that great, Mom?"

"Um-hum, it's great."

I stood and took a deep breath of the warm sunshine.

He took my hand again and together we slushed our way back through the growing puddle and up the steps.

At the door, he turned.

"I think I'll stay out some more," he said. "Okay?"

"Okay, but you'd better stay away from the biggest puddles."

"Awright Mom."

He was gone, descending the steps with noisy bounds.

"Hey, Bonnie," his call had to reach two back yards away. "I showed my mom our first spring flower."

I went in and removed my boots, then felt for the hanger on the closet floor.

Pity? All I knew about it was that it was a four letter word—one that I didn't really need.

No one will ever know all the wonderful things that I have been shown, since I lost my sight.

A Matter of Trust

The persistent ringing of the telephone drew Marion Blake from her place of contentment beneath the warm blankets. Uneasily she groped for her robe and hastened toward the bedroom door. She hated it when the phone rang at night. It always made her heart beat crazily for fear of what might be wrong. Probably a wrong number she tried to convince herself, as she glanced toward the digital clock. It was no longer Halloween night she realized; now the date was November first, one fifteen in the morning. Who would call at such an hour! She barely avoided banging her shin on a chair, left carelessly away from the kitchen table, and reached the phone as it gave another disturbing demand for attention. Bill slept on. She had often declared that he wouldn't waken if a locomotive ran through the bedroom. He proved it again now. She hoped the children would continue to sleep. She felt not only fear but anger as she lifted the receiver and spoke a curt "Yes?" into the mouthpiece.

A male voice spoke from the other end and drew the

last bit of sleepiness from her.

"Mrs. Blake?"

"Yes," she was hesitant now.

"This is Sergeant Collins down at the Police Station. We have your boy, Randall, in custo—"

"But there must be some mistake," she interrupted.

Annoyance again took hold of her. The lateness of the call, scaring her half to death, and now the police—saying Randy was out. No apology, nothing—and all because they hadn't checked things out. The annoyance was conveyed to her voice.

"I'm afraid you've made a mistake," she said again. "It's not our Randy. He's in bed—asleep."

There was silence for a moment; then the male voice responded.

"I see. Would you check that please, Ma'am?"

"What do you mean?"

"Check Randall's bed, Ma'am." It was an order.

"But—" She felt angry now.

"I'll wait, Ma'am," the unrelenting voice demanded.

She laid the phone down rather noisily and went toward Randy's room. Of course, Randy was in bed. He had gone to bed shortly after nine. They had always insisted that their kids stay in on Halloween so that they wouldn't get involved in any of the goings-on. Even though Randy was eighteen, and in his final year of high school, he still respected the authority of his parents and had never given them any trouble. Now Jerry, his younger brother, had them a bit concerned at times. He had a much more determined streak, but so far no major problems. Marcie was still young enough to be quite pliable.

She felt like a goose, checking Randy's room, but the sergeant had insisted and she would have to be able to say truthfully that she had.

She opened his door quietly and refused to admit, even

to herself, that her heart was beating even more wildly. Was that relief that she felt in seeing the form beneath the blankets? Something compelled her to move over to the bed. Perhaps it was her love and thankfulness toward her son that again he had not let them down. She reached down to lay a hand gently on the sleeping form, but as her hand touched the blanket she realized that something was wrong. There was not the firmness that there should have been. Only softness lay beneath her hand. She reached for the light and switched it on. The bed was empty, save for pillows and blankets arranged to—yes, arranged—deliberately— Her head spun. A cold breeze fluttered the draperies and drew her eyes to the window. It had been left partly open. He had left by way of the window. She couldn't understand it. Somehow it all didn't fit. Randy had said he felt tired and had gone to bed early. Big test the next day, he had said. She hadn't doubted—not for one moment. He had said—her head reeled. Finally she remembered what had brought her to Randy's room. The phone—and the police sergeant was waiting. She almost staggered as she made her way back to the kitchen.

Marcie called from her room.

"What's wrong, Mom?"

"It's okay, Dear. Go back to sleep. I'll—I'll tell you all about it—in the morning." She managed to reply with a fairly steady voice.

Slowly she picked up the receiver. Her voice was shaky now, like the hand that held the phone.

"He's not there—"

The caller didn't seem at all surprised.

"If you and your husband would like to come down and pick him up—"

"What'd he do?"

"A little Halloween activity got out of hand. But we

can discuss that when you get here."

"Yes—of course—we'll—we'll be right down."

She hung up the phone and stood trembling. Her boy—at the police station—taking part in Halloween activities—a little "out of hand," the man said. Oh, no, not Randy. What would it mean? What had he done? Would it be serious? She couldn't believe it—she just couldn't. She had been so sure of Randy—so proud. He had been such a model son. Why, she would have trusted him—trusted him completely—but he had tricked them and lied and now. . . .

The tears began to fall. The lying was what hurt the most. She felt betrayed—so used—so crushed by it. If only he hadn't lied. If he had just openly defied them and walked out and slammed the door—but this—this.

She leaned her head against the wall and let the sobs overtake her. She must pull herself together and go waken Bill.

"Oh Randy—why?"—but there didn't seem to be any answer.

Bill was silent on the way to the police station. He had pulled himself up wide-eyed when she woke him and tried to explain in a rather jumbled fashion, combined with tears, what had just transpired. When he finally seemed to have it somewhat straight in his mind, he had flung back the covers and risen to hurriedly dress. His eyes looked troubled. He pulled his jacket on, then turned to Marion and seemed surprised to see that she was dressed also. He took a step toward her, seeing the hurt in her eyes, and pulled her close. He held her for a moment, saying nothing. Indeed, there was no need for words. Finally he released her.

"You needn't come."

"I'm coming. I can't just wait here."

He said no more and she knew that he understood that she had to go.

"Crazy, fool kid," she heard him mutter, and they left silently together and remained silent until they pulled up in front of the police station. Other cars were there, and Marion realized that they were not the only parents who had been awakened from sleep to come down here to get—but it was different with them. Randy was not a rowdy teenager. He was not a law breaker. He—but then—why were they here? "Oh, God," she sobbed and bowed her head to her hands.

"You can wait in the car," Bill was saying. "We shouldn't be long."

She did not respond, but was only too glad to stay where she was.

The Franklins came out the door—but they were always having trouble with Billie—"Butch" the kids all called him. She hoped that Randy hadn't been involved with "Butch" Franklin. How silly, she scolded herself. Here she was still fighting to protect him as though he were a two-year-old instead of eighteen and deceitful.

It seemed forever until Bill and Randy came out of the door. Randy silently crawled in the back, and Bill slid behind the wheel. Bill spoke.

"I suggest that we all need some sleep and a bit of time to think and pray before we go into this. We'll talk it all out in the morning."

When Bill used that tone of voice, the whole family knew that it was final. She said nothing—nor did Randy—but her heart was crying out against him. For the first time since she had held him in pride as a tiny baby—her first-born—she felt resentment and anger toward him.

"How could you—how could you—lie and cheat and and let us down? Oh God, how could he? He knows how we have raised him to be truthful and upright. He knows it's a sin—"

Fear struck at her heart. They had felt that everything was all right between this son that they loved and his God, but was it? True, he faithfully attended all of the services of the church, had been baptized, took communion, led in the Youth Fellowship, testified to his friends—but were all of those things simply a cover-up for an emptiness within?

"Oh, God," her prayer changed, "don't let him be lost. I know that Satan desires him . . . that he would lead him astray. But don't let it happen, Lord. Still, Lord . . . he knows . . . he knows that lying is sinful, that . . . ."

A still small voice interrupted her. "Have you always responded to what I have showed you? What makes you feel so superior or holy? Have you never sinned? Have you always obeyed my promptings? Have you never been tripped up by envy, jealousy, materialism, gossip—? What makes you so sure that his sin is worse than your own?"

Marion's spirit was humbled. "God forgive me; forgive me. I promise, with your help, to try harder. Help me not to sit in judgment, Lord."

Still the problem was unresolved. Her boy had lied and deceived them; he was in trouble with the law, and her heart was broken. What will the people of the church say? Ugly self-pride raised the question. She tried to push it aside, but it persisted. They had been so sure of Randy, and now—she would never be able to trust him again.

Tears filled her eyes. How hurtful it was to have one's trust betrayed.

They reached home and, in silence, entered the house. A wall had quickly and insurmountably sprung up between them.

In the soft light of the kitchen she saw Randy's determined jaw and defiant eyes. She had never seen that expression on his face before. She turned away from it, lest she could no longer keep from angrily striking out at him in a wild torrent of hurtful words.

"Go to bed," Bill said in a tired, defeated-sounding voice.

Randy turned to go, his chin held high, his step showing his resentment.

She turned to go to her room. Again she went through the motions of preparing herself for sleep, but she was sure that there would be no more sleep for her that night.

Morning finally arrived. She lay staring at the ceiling. Her eyes ached from lack of sleep and even her body felt stiff and sore from lying in bed without being allowed to relax. Still, her sharpest hurt was deep within her. She felt so defeated, so cheated of all that was rightfully due her. She had been a good mother, she had trained him carefully and been a proper example to him, and now—he had let her down so dreadfully.

Bill stirred. She marvelled that he had somehow been able to get back to sleep. She knew that he, too, had been deeply hurt. He leaned over and pulled her close for a moment and placed a kiss on her cheek. There was nothing unusual about that. It was the way that he greeted her every morning. She often smiled about it. As soon as he awakened, he pulled her close and kissed her, with eyes only half open. He let the kiss fall where it may—on her forehead, her cheek, her nose, her chin—occasionally, he even managed to find her lips.

He opened his eyes a little wider now and simply said, "Hi."

She blinked. Just like that. "Hi." As though the whole world hadn't fallen apart sometime during the night. He kissed her again. This time the kiss landed where it was intended. His eyes darkened and she knew that he remembered what had happened and what was still ahead.

He held her in silence for a moment and then began to speak slowly, quietly. "Apparently Randy left his room by way of his window last night and joined some of his school friends. They figured it would be their last Halloween together so they decided that they should 'do' something. They met other kids on the street and one thing led to another. Some of the rowdier kids were involved in damaging road signs and some windows. The sergeant said that they were sure that Randy and his friends were not responsible for any of that."

He hesitated, then went on. "They did get some spray paint, though, and messed up one wall of the school. The sergeant said he couldn't make any promises; it'll have to go before the court. But he's going to recommend that, rather than charge the boys, they be made to buy paint and repaint the wall that they sprayed the paint on. He thinks the court will go for it. If so, the boys will be mighty lucky that they met up with a policeman willing to give them a break. It was a dumb, fool thing to do, but they are boys . . . ."

Marion could understand that. Of course, they were boys and could easily get involved more than they had intended, but to deliberately plan ahead to deceive his parents, and to lie to cover the deceit—she found it very difficult to forgive Randy for that.

"Well, I guess we'd better go face it," Bill said, and releasing her he threw back the covers and got up to do just that.

She placed her feet on the floor too, almost amazed that they still held her.

"We may as well have our chat before we call the other two," Bill said. "We'll talk to Randy in his room."

"Providing he's still there," she said bitterly.

"Now, Mother," Bill cautioned. "I know that the boy has let us down, but there's a lot of good in him yet. I hope he can profit from this experience and—"

"But he lied," she fairly hissed. "He lied and cheated. I'll never be able to trust him again—never."

Bill looked at her evenly. He seemed to be searching for words, not sure just which ones to choose.

"Of course you will," he finally said with emphasis. "He's made a bad mistake. What I am concerned with now is how he is going to respond, now that he realizes what he has done. If he is sorry, if he learns, then I don't think that we need to fear the same mistake again."

Marion said nothing, but inwardly she still cried out that the trust that she had felt so completely had been shattered—too shattered to be gathered up and repaired.

When they entered Randy's room they found him already awake. He didn't look like he'd had any more sleep than his mother. Marion noticed that the defiance was gone. An embarrassed, defeated look had taken its place. He didn't wait for them to say anything.

"I know—I know," he blurted out. "I was stupid, an' I'm sorry."

Bill sat down.

"Yeah," he said evenly. "You were stupid. What we want to know is, why?"

He left the question hanging there suspended. Randy waited a minute, then started talking slowly; but as he talked, his words gathered momentum and his voice cracked on occasion.

"I've never been able to do anything with the fellows from school. They do all sorts of things, an' then talk about them an' laugh an' slap one another on the back an' have a great time. An' I've always been on the outside, a real jam-tart—they think I'm a real odd-ball. Well, I've never cared about the drinkin' an' smokin' or pot or anything, nor the stories they tell about girls, or . . . but sometimes it's not bad things that they do, just fun things, but I've never been able to do any of that either. I've always just had to stand back an'—well, you don't know what it's like. Anyway, the guys decided to have a little fun our last year an' all, and they asked me to come too. I couldn't believe it, that they'd want me, but they did. An' how—how could I say, 'My Mom an' Dad won't let me,'—eighteen, an' they still won't let me out at night. I couldn't, I just couldn't."

His voice broke in a sob.

"I know—I know I did wrong—an' I'm sorry."

He was sorry. Marion knew that as she saw the broad shoulders of her grown son shake. Had they put too many restrictions on him? Had they held him too tightly? She had never realized before the pressures that he had been under, the desire to look normal in the eyes of the other kids at school.

"Son," Bill placed a hand on the shaking shoulder. "Son, we can understand all of that and if we have been wrong, we're sorry. We have wanted to protect you from things like what happened last night—not to confine you—because we love you."

"I know Dad. I know."

"We accept your apology," Bill went on. "But remember you have hurt Someone else by your actions last night as well. I think that you had better straighten out some things with Him too."

"I have—all night I have."

"Good."

That was all. Bill stood to leave and Marion knew that he considered the incident closed.

Randy looked across at her, reading the hurt in her eyes.

"I'm sorry, Mom," he said in a husky voice.

She shook her head, the tears spilling down her cheeks

silently. She knew that he meant it sincerely, and she turned to go.

It was with thankfulness that she heard his apology, with true deep feelings that she rejoiced over the fact that he had asked forgiveness of his God. Still, her heart ached within her. She wondered how many times in the future she might check his room to see if he really was there as he had said he would be, how many times doubts would enter her mind when he said something as a fact—how many times—

What a sad thing it was to lose one's trust. She had trusted him so completely, but now— She prayed that the day might soon come when she would feel that she could trust him again, but inwardly she knew that it would be a long, difficult road.

Son

Son,
I love you.
I love you—though I scarce know how to show it.

It used to be so easy.
I'd cuddle you close and kiss you
As often as I felt inclined,
And sometimes that was "often."

And then you started "growing up."
But even then you'd still permit
A hug or a kiss on the forehead
When I said goodnight.

But now, that too is gone
For you're a teenager now
And anything like hugs or kisses
Or even tender words
Is "so silly."
And embarrassing.
So—"Momish."

And yet I love you
Just as much
Or maybe more.
Sometimes I feel so proud
And all choked up inside
When I see you shoulder responsibility
And even show your independence.

You'll make it, Son.
You're doing okay.
You make me proud.
I love you.

But I can only "be there."
And smile.
No hugs.
Or kisses.
These have to wait.

I'll wait.
My love will keep me patient.
You see, I know deep down inside
Someday it'll be okay again.

Someday—when you feel sure of manhood—
When I'm Grandma to your children,
Yes—you'll think of me as "dear old Mom."
And when you come
Or go,
You'll kiss me and give me a hug
And maybe you'll even say,
"Mom—I love you."

Mommy, You Come with Me

(A personal experience of the author)

The morning was a dark, cloudy one—too dark for my three-year-old son to feel safe to venture forth alone. Only his desire for a playmate would cause him to consider such a seemingly risky trip. Bravely he opened the door, looked about, and stepped out onto the back step—then he turned back, eyes big, and hurriedly closed the door behind him.

"Mommy," he said, "it might snow on me."

I turned from the ironing board and assured him that I didn't think it would snow—it was just a cloudy day, that was all.

He sat down on the inside step to think about this for a while, then another thought came to him.

"Mommy," he said, "will you take me to Karen's house?"

"No, Mommy can't go," I answered him, thinking of his two-month-old twin brothers. "I have to stay with the babies."

He pulled himself up and bravely made another attempt, but with the same result. Again he came back and carefully closed the door tightly behind him.

"Mommy—please, will you take me to Karen's

house?'' A new thought was added, ''And then you can run right back home again—fast—to the babies.''

I went to him then. ''Mommy can't come with you, but Jesus will go with you.''

The little face turned to mine suddenly lit up, ''Mommy,'' he said, ''you come with me and let Jesus take care of the babies.''

For a moment I was stunned, though I had to turn from him to hide the smile that showed on my face. How could I answer him? Would I trust one child to Jesus' care and not the other two? Certainly not! It was just that the babies were far more dependent than my little man of three. The day would come when they too would be guided to take forward steps—often alone. The steps were at times difficult for a child and for Mother. As a mother I knew he could not always be sheltered and coddled. I put my arm around him.

''Honey,'' I said, ''would you like us to pray and ask Jesus to go with you?''

''A-huh,'' was his answer.

After our prayer I opened the door for him. How good it was to know that it was true—though I couldn't always be there with him, Jesus could. I wanted him to know this too. He looked around, and then started off.

''Mommy will be at the window,'' I called after him.

I watched him go with tears in my eyes. He was brave, my little man; he was afraid—but he was brave. I smiled at his exaggerated erectness, his overly quick steps. I knew exactly how he felt. Just before he rounded the corner, he stopped to wave one last time . . . and I, from my kitchen window, waved back. Then he turned again and was gone.

''Little boy,'' my heart whispered, ''this morning you have gone a lot further than just to Karen's house. You have taken another big step toward becoming a man.''

A Son Is Born

He rubbed his hands as he entered the room,
  For the morning air held a chill.
A faint smile flicked on the time-worn face;
  She knew he had something to tell.

Slowly he stretched out his hands to the fire,
  The warmth seemed to loosen his tongue;
"Remember the young man who stopped by last night,
  After the "NO ROOM" was hung?"

She nodded, remembering the earnest young face;
  The eyes seemed to plead for some way.
"I told them to bed in the stable," he said;
  "They took it—slept there in the hay."

"A son was born to the couple last night."
  "A son!" and the old lady smiled,
Knowing the joy of the young woman's heart,
  The joy that accompanies a child.

"I must fix the young woman a warm drink," she said.
  "Yes, that would be good," said the man.
"A son," she repeated, enjoying the words,
  Then she set to work on her plan.

"I wonder what they will name the wee babe;
  They'll choose some name of the kin."
Then she placed the drink in an earthen jar
  And journeyed forth from the inn.

The withered man and his aged wife
  Shared the joy that a baby brings.
But, ah! They missed much, for they did not know
  That the Babe was the King of Kings.

The Easter Story

(An Easter story as it could have been told—not as the writer understands the teaching of Scripture in all cases.)

Gather 'round me now, all you young uns, and I'll tell you the Easter story. Ole Gramps may not have much book-learnin' but I shore do know what Easter's all about. And, you know, I think thet it is the most important thing in the world thet you know what it's all about too.

One day God looked down from His Heaven and His heart was very sad. There were all His children sinnin' and carryin' on somethin' awful. God shook His mighty head and tears washed down His cheeks. He loved His children, but they were a choosin' sin instead of righteousness, and self instead of God.

"What can we do?" God asked. "I told 'em plainly, 'The soul thet sinneth, it shall die.' There's nothin' thet I can do to change thet. They've made their choice—and they didn't choose me. They're lost. There's nothin' thet I can do to save 'em now."

God hung His head in heaviness of heart. Justice must be done. The punishment for sin was death.

"Jest a minute," said the Holy Spirit. "Let me go down and speak to 'em and show 'em their great sinfulness."

"Thet is good," said God. "They should realize their sinfulness. But even if they do, there'd be no way back—they still must pay fer their sin. And the penalty is death."

"I'll go, Father." The Son stepped forward quietly. I'll go—and die fer 'em—in their place. Then the penalty will be paid as required."

God looked at His only Son. Love filled His eyes and heart.

"But you, as Holy God, can't go down into sin—or die."

"Then—then, I'll go as man."

"As man . . ." God thought long. "Yes—as man you could go. But, my Son, do you realize the price? Even I could not be with you when you die fer 'em. You'd need to do it all alone."

Softly the Son replied, "Yes, I know, but it's the only way. And we must save 'em—we must. It's the *only* way."

And so He came—as a tiny baby-child born of Mary, and laid in a manger-bed. God had to stand back and let the Mighty Creator of the universe cry fer His feedin' and wait fer Mary to lift His head from its pillow.

God watched Him as He grew and He was pleased with Him. But His heart was heavy, too, fer as the earth-years passed one by one, the Son's *hour* drew closer and closer.

He grew to be a man and a leader of the people. Long hours were spent in healin' and helpin'. Not many followed Him but the few who did knew thet He was no ord'nary man. There were others, *followers,* who would have made Him their king. They liked the way thet He put the religious leaders in their place, provided bread when they were hungry and healed their sick bodies. But Jesus knew thet His task was not to establish a force to chase Roman soldiers from the land.

Then *the day* came. God watched His Son walk slowly to the Garden. The Son's steps were heavy fer He too knew thet His *hour* was at hand. God heard His prayer. He saw the drops of blood. He felt the pain of the Son's heart, His dread of death.

God watched in agony as His Son struggled with temptation, then sank back in relief when He heard, "Not my will, but Thine be done."

"Go," God said to His angels. "Go to Him." And then went swoopin' down from Heaven—fast as the lightnin'—and into the Garden they went, where they gently lifted Him up and wiped the blood-sweat from His brow.

Then came hours of bitter sufferin' fer the Son was mocked and beaten and finally led to Calvary. All Heaven shook when He fell beneath the cross; and when the burly Simon lifted it to his own shoulders, the recordin' angel lifted his pen to make special note in his book.

The heavy blows of the wooden hammers thudded out the message, "He's gonna die. He's gonna die." And then the wooden cross was dropped, with a sickenin' 'thud', into position. God reached forth suddenly, as though to lift His Son from the tree, and then His eyes fell on the mockin', half-crazed mob crowdin' 'round, shoutin' words of blasphemy and hate. Oh, how sinful they were. Surely they deserved to die. And yet love—unreasonable love fer 'em—swept through the Almighty, and God pulled back His hand. The sins of the world must be atoned. His Son—His only Son—must bear 'em all . . . alone.

God watched His sinless Son as He hung suspended between earth and heaven. He saw the pain in His eyes, the trickles of blood on His brow, the ragged tears in the flesh of His hands thet sent searin' pain reachin' from His fingertips to His shoulders. He could bear no more.

God turned His back, and the thunders rolled across the heavens. "I cannot watch Him die—nor will they," God cried, and all of the earth was darkened.

The long hours dragged by, and finally the time came when the Son gave up the ghost. His body sagged on the tree. It was finished! The price fer sinners' salvation was paid! God turned back to His Son and longin' filled His heart. His all-knowin' eyes saw the few who stood weepin' at the cross and those who came and tearfully prepared the body fer buryin'. He watched also as runnin' feet hurried to the tomb on thet *great mornin'*.

And then all the angels of Heaven gathered 'round, fer somethin' great was about to be discovered. The Son was no longer in the tomb. He had risen like He had said He would. Surely the whole earth would rejoice—the mountains and valleys would echo with allelujahs, shouts of praise would reach to the very stars. But no—only silence—silence and the world-crowd's usual busyness.

Was it worth it after all? And then Mighty God looked beyond the crowded streets and hurryin' throngs into a few hearts of the Son's faithful followers, and God saw there what He wanted to see. There was joy thet the Son had risen—joy thet they too could rise to be with Him. Their joy bubbled up, and they ran to share it with others.

Then God looked forward and saw Peter, no more cowerin' in a corner because of a young girl's remark, but standin' boldly before a crowd of temple-goers and proclaimin' thet the price of sin had been paid, thet they needed to believe and repent. And many did—and the small band of followers grew. And God saw Stephen, crumblin' before His murderers, leavin' a testimony fer time and eternity; and God saw Paul, pushin' his way across the land declarin' the good news wherever he went; and God saw Philip and Bartholomew, Timothy and Onesimus, Goforth and Livingstone, you and me.

And God smiled and sat back contented. Then He waved to summon the angels. "Prepare all Heaven," He cried, "My Son is coming home." But as the angels swooped up to do His biddin' God spoke again. "No, not the victory feast. Not yet. We'll wait until *all* my children are home and then we'll celebrate together."

The banners waved, the trumpets rang out, and God stood to welcome His Son back into His rightful place. After a long and tender embrace, He turned the Son to look back down on the world thet He had just left behind.

"Look, Son. You were right. It worked. See him . . . and see him . . . and see her over there. She'll soon be joinin' us. And see him. He's ready to lay down his life fer the Gospel. And look at her. And thet little one. Oh, Son—just look. *Just look!* We'd better hurry. We have mansions to prepare. They'll be comin'—before we know it—and we want everythin' to be ready. Jest think, Son. It worked. They'll be here with us fer all eternity."

And the Father and the Son joined in joyous laughter, and all of Heaven rang with the sound.

Emmaus

Triumphant!
The victory is secured.
The work is done.
The mission has been accomplished.
Redemption is completed.
What He has come to do
He has done.
He can rejoice.
IT IS FINISHED.

IT IS FINISHED.
He is the victor
Over sin
And death.

IT IS FINISHED.
He has died—victorious.
He has risen—triumphant.
He can return to the Father.

IT IS FINISHED.

Or is it?

Two walk alone,
Confused, discouraged, tired, defeated.
The long road stretches out before them,
The rumbling city behind,
And on the hill a used cross
And in the garden a sealed tomb.
He was to be . . .
It should have been . . .
We thought He was . . .
We loved Him.
Triumphant?
What did He come to do?
To die—He did that.
To rise again—Yes, and that.
To love—Ah, yes—to love,
Not just 'til death,
To love
And love, forever.

And so, the victorious, triumphant Saviour
Walked again a dusty road,
Fellowshiped with weary travelers,
Broke coarse bread in a humble home,
To teach, to empathize, to love,
Because?
Because He's Jesus.
He came to love
. . . to show compassion
. . . to be concerned.

His death didn't change Him,
His resurrection didn't alter Him.
His ascension hasn't affected Him.
He's Jesus.
He's still there to teach,
To heal,
To hold us steady,
To fill our need,
To love.

Our redemption is complete.
IT IS FINISHED.
But Jesus isn't.
He's still at work,
Listening to broken hearts,
Walking dusty roads,
Binding up wounds,
Putting lives back together,
Giving hope and love.

Yesterday . . . today . . . forever . . .
That same Jesus.
HE IS NOT FINISHED!
Never!
As long as we need Him.

An Apple for the Teacher

It wasn't a very big apple, nor was it a very nice one. In fact it was rather wizened, and the red of its once-full cheeks appeared to have stayed with it simply because it had no other place to go.

Miss Marianne Carver looked past the apple and the little grimy hand that held it outstretched, at the eager face of the eight-year-old. It was a thin face, a little pale, and accumulated dirt and coal dust showed that it had not recently felt soap and water. The face was framed by long unkempt curly hair that made one wonder if it might not be pretty if washed and brushed. But the viewer would hardly notice these things, for the eyes seemed to draw like a magnet and hold her gaze.

They were beautiful deep-blue eyes and they were too large, too blue, and far too eager, as they met Miss Carver's eyes now. Everything in life seemed to depend upon the outcome of the next few moments.

Suddenly Miss Marianne Carver found her thoughts

going back to things which she had supposed were long ago buried and forgotten. She didn't wish to recall them even now, but her mind refused to leave them in the past.

Hers hadn't been an easy life, nor a pleasant one. Not that her state was any different, or any worse, than the rest of the children in the small lumber town. They all shared the same dilemma, the same emptiness of stomach, the same need for warmer clothes.

The mill was shut down.

There was no work for even those who wished to find it —but there was drink. There was always drink for those who wished to choose this way of forgetting that they had hungry little ones at home with feet protruding through worn shoes that let in the wet sloshy snow.

Her father was one of these—no work, a bed-ridden wife, and a family of eight whose stomachs demanded to be fed even though the small grocery store would allow no more credit.

It was a sad, hungry village that survived only on hope, for each of the sixty-eight lumbermen who dwelt there repeatedly told themselves and one another that soon the mill would re-open, soon there would be jobs for all, soon there would be money aplenty to make up to their families for the things they had been doing without. Hope—but hope didn't put a meal on the table or mend worn shoes. Soon—but "soon" never did seem to get one day closer.

There was in the village a small undenominational church. The elderly man who ministered to the people, with the help of his equally elderly wife, shared with the people the hunger, the cold, and the hope.

Whenever possible they would pass out a little assistance here or there, sharing their own meager supplies.

But they, too, lived from day to day, not always knowing where the next meal was coming from, calmly assuring others, as they gave away their last bit of flour, that God always provides.

About the only other thing that the village offered its young was school. Here you could go and in the eagerness of learning, forget momentarily that your stomach had had very little for breakfast.

The most wonderful thing about school was the teacher. Marianne saw the teacher as someone from another world—a fairy-book princess—a goddess.

She, Miss Gertrude Fairmore, represented different things to different people. Some thought of her as a walking advertisement of the world of fashions. Others saw her as a soft employee of the government, who was able to pick up a monthly paycheck that would have cared for the needs of several families, but which she could spend at her pleasure. Others saw her as a spoiled child of a "wealthy" family who was able to "edjecate" her and give her such an enviable and elevated position in society.

Yes, Miss Gertrude Fairmore was a "special" person in the village. Some looked down on her in jealousy and contempt. Others looked up to her in envy and admiration. But little Marianne Carver just sat and looked and dreamed.

Miss Fairmore wore beautiful things and Marianne would look at the softness and brightness of them, then back again to her own dirty, wrinkled, ragged article that somewhat resembled a dress. The contrast made her almost cry.

Miss Fairmore always smelled good. Marianne liked to have her near, so that she might enjoy the odor of perfume that accompanied her. It was so different from the other people with whom Marianne had contact.

Miss Fairmore had dark hair that shone. Marianne looked about the room with its many heads bent over the desks. There were many colors, but the condition was the same—dull from being unwashed and scruffy-looking from being untamed. Marianne would look again to the shining, carefully-styled hair of Miss Fairmore and sigh a deep sigh. Marianne longed to touch that glistening hair, but she knew better than to try. Even though she was just a child, she was much aware of the fact that Miss Fairmore would draw back should she venture too near.

Still, how she loved her, how she wished to please her. To Marianne, Miss Fairmore represented everything that was to be desired. And then one day it happened—

It wasn't a very big apple, nor was it a very nice one. In fact, it was rather wizened, and the red of its once-full cheeks appeared to have stayed with it simply because it had no other place to go.

Marianne was proud as she held it out—proud and eager. Now, surely Miss Fairmore would know how much she loved her.

The other kids had all quickly devoured the apples given to them by the kind minister, but Marianne had carefully preserved hers in her scarf for her beloved teacher.

She fairly trembled with eagerness as she held it out.

"It's for you," she whispered.

She looked up into Miss Fairmore's face, expecting to find surprise and delight.

Miss Fairmore didn't look delighted at all. In fact, she looked displeased and perhaps a trifle angry. Marianne thought that there must be a mistake. Miss Fairmore must not realize that the apple was for her. She held it closer. Miss Fairmore pushed at the apple and sniffed her displeasure.

"Take it away at once, Marianne," she said sternly, "and don't bring it near my desk again. And look at your hands; they're filthy."

With this last hiss of contempt, Miss Fairmore busied herself with wiping her hand that had pushed the apple away, with a dainty lace handkerchief. She turned stiffly away, and the little girl fled the room in a torrent of tears.

The deep hurt changed her feelings for Miss Fairmore. In fact, it changed her feelings about all of life. One goal became hers—to be a teacher so that she, too, might shun whomever she desired. She'd have education, she'd have fine clothes and perfume, she'd get a paycheck each month, and she'd carry herself proud and aloof.

Bitter, hard years followed. Marianne put herself to the task. She took all of the schooling that she could at the village school, then left home and went to the city. It wasn't easy going to school by day and working graveyard shift in a downtown cafe at night, but she made it.

All through the lean hard years she kept the goal in view. Someday she'd be in a position to snub the world; they'd know that she was a person to be admired but not touched.

Finally, she was through. She felt that she owned the world as the monthly paychecks came in. She thoroughly weighed every purchase—was it the best? Was it to be envied? Her eyes glittered at the purchase of each fashionable new dress. Her wardrobe filled, but her life remained empty.

One day, as she stood looking into her mirror, she saw looking back at her a fashionable young woman with shining well-groomed hair, a carefully made-up face, and cold uphappy eyes. Desperately, she tried to hide it from herself, but she knew that it was true.

"It's this place," she told herself. So she applied to go east—anywhere in the east—the next school term.

The east—she expected to find here only enchantment, historical sights, splendor. What a shock it had been, when she arrived, to discover that she had been assigned to a small coal-mining town—and business had been poor.

The shabbiness of it, the squalor of some of the homes, and the distinctive and nauseating smells filled her with such a distaste as to border on illness.

From week through miserable week, she held her head high and her skirts close to her to keep from brushing against those with whom she must associate.

In a way she felt pleasure. Never had she felt more like Miss Gertrude Fairmore.

She'd show these slummers that there were better things in life.

She dressed in her finest clothing, brushed her hair till it shone, and wore fragrant scents that told of richness. Deliberately, she packed elaborate lunches for school and carelessly tossed large unfinished portions away while hungry eyes watched longingly.

She was reaping her revenge at life and savoring it as a tasty morsel. And now, here was her chance for a glorious victory, for before her stood the dirty, hungry little girl with the outstretched, wrinkled apple.

Do it—say it—she urged herself on. And then she looked into the pitiful face, at the eager pleading eyes, and saw once again the scene of long ago.

Strange—she also saw something else. Her accomplishment hadn't brought her as much pleasure as she had hoped. Deep within her was a lonely aching heart, needing someone to love. Too high and too strong had been the wall that she had built; no one had been able to penetrate it. Before her now was not just a dirty, unkempt little girl, but a warm affectionate child.

Suddenly, she was on her knees holding the child close,

while sobs caught in her throat. But the big empty hurt was gone from her heart.

She stroked the tangled curly hair and finally, when she found control, she whispered softly.

"Thank you, Mary. Thank you for the apple. Thank you—for love."

Sin in the Camp

Lazily the clouds drifted southward, while the warm fall sun lifted the heads of the few remaining flowers by the walk.

"What a beautiful day," mused Beth Robinson as she watched a convoy of fall leaves follow one another across her front lawn. She stood at her front window enjoying the scene before her, when suddenly her attention was turned to a moving van pulling up to the vacant house next door.

At once excitement surged through her.

"Our new neighbors," she said to herself. "I wonder just what they will be like. I can hardly wait to find out."

She didn't have long to wait, for just behind the moving van drove a station wagon. Beth watched as a neatly dressed woman of about thirty—no, maybe closer to thirty-five—climbed out of the car and stood looking at her new home. She seemed quite satisfied, for she turned to the man who had walked around from the driver's side of the car, and smiled.

Together they walked toward the white house with its yellow trim and neatly-clipped front lawn.

Beth Robinson was so intent on watching the couple that she almost missed seeing the children who had somehow reached the front door ahead of their parents.

They were wild with excitement, jumping up and down and clamoring for the door to be opened so that they might explore their new domain. The girl looked the oldest, probably ten or so, and the tow-haired boy with the freckles looked about seven or eight. The little dark fellow was likely a pre-schooler.

The door was opened, and the children rushed in followed closely by their parents.

The phone rang and Beth went to answer it. It was Mildred Greene from across the street.

"I see our new neighbors have arrived."

"Oh yes. They look like very nice folk. My Tom will be disappointed that they don't have a boy his age. He's missed David so much since he moved away."

"I was wondering about inviting them to church."

"I plan to drop in a little later today to see if I can be of any help, so I'll ask."

The conversation continued about the coming Sunday School advance in which both ladies had an active part, but Beth followed along halfheartedly. Her eyes were on the movers as they made their trips from van to house, so she found it hard to keep her mind on what Mildred was saying. Finally she mumbled something about having to get lunch on for Fred and excused herself from the phone, promising to call back later.

All morning Beth was full of thoughts of the new neighbors. She found herself watching the proceedings next door to see what "clues" she could gather to tell her what kind of folks they would be.

The children, like any normal children, seemed to be highly excited with it all—perhaps even a little on the wild side, Beth thought.

"That middle fellow with the freckles might be a bit of a problem in a Sunday School class. The girl seems quiet enough—almost shy. It takes all of her time to keep the little guy out of the way of the movers."

Beth smiled to herself.

"A real little mother," she noted. "She'll be good for my Sylvia."

When Fred came for lunch, Beth was full of news of the new neighbors.

"I'm going right over after lunch to see if I can be of any help."

"You should have invited them for lunch. I'm sure that that would have helped."

Beth looked up in surprise.

"That many? Besides, I'm not ready for company."

"Neither is she—but you're going over there."

Beth looked annoyed and turned back to the stove. What did men know about such things anyway?

After Fred had left for work, Beth waited for awhile to give her new neighbor a chance to get a few things in order. Then, after slipping into a crisp summery dress, she ventured across her back lawn.

Her knock at the door was answered promptly by the woman herself.

"Hi," Beth said easily. "I'm Beth Robinson from next door. Welcome to the neighborhood."

"Thank you," the woman smiled. "I'm Marie Wilson, and this is my husband Jim."

After the acknowledgments, Beth offered her services.

"That's very kind of you," Marie said appreciatively, "but there really isn't much to do except put things away and I almost need to do that myself so that I know where to find them again. Would you join us for a cup of coffee? We didn't stop for lunch. The children went over to the corner hamburger stand."

"You have three?" Beth queried.

"Yes, Judy is ten; Thomas or Tommy, as he is usually known, is eight; and Gary will be five next month."

"We have two. Sylvia is eleven; our Tom is thirteen. He was hoping that our new neighbors would have a boy his age. He misses David so much. He's the boy who used to live here. They were wonderful folks—the Betts."

"Yes, we've met them."

"We'd be very happy to have you folks take their place in our church as well as in their home. It's the church just down Thirty-Fifth a couple of blocks—Faith Church."

"I'm afraid that we haven't been too faithful in our church attendance, but it would be good for the children. Perhaps we'll be able to go on Sunday to sort of help the children get acquainted in their new neighborhood."

"That would be nice," Beth responded. "Now I must run. I had my lunch such a short while ago that I won't join you for coffee this time, but thank you. Remember, if there is any way that we can help out, we'd be happy to."

Beth hurried home, anxious to let Mildred know that the new neighbors had promised to attend church on Sunday.

The Wilsons kept their word and on Sunday morning took their place with the worshippers at Faith Church. Because the people were friendly and the children felt at home, the Wilsons decided to return again the following Sunday.

"Besides," said Jim Wilson to his wife, "this is our town now, and we need to get acquainted with the people."

She agreed. But, down inside, both of them knew that there was something lacking in their lives and they hoped that somehow the church might have the answer.

Five Sundays slipped by. The Wilsons hadn't missed a one, and each Sunday brought added interest and a feeling of getting nearer to the end of the search. As yet, they weren't quite sure what it was that they needed. But the church people knew and much prayer was going up on behalf of the Wilsons. In fact, some lips were already poised to offer a prayer of thanks for their conversion. Then something happened.

It was Beth Robinson who saw it first. Being the closest neighbor of the Wilsons, she knew almost all of their doings, and she kept the ladies' prayer group informed so that they would know how to pray.

It was a clear, almost crisp, fall morning when Beth looked up from her kitchen sink to see the milkman leave his truck. He was quite a "usual" milkman, a little friendlier than most perhaps; but then, he'd delivered milk to them for eight or ten years, and you sort of got to know one another by then. Burt was what everyone called him. Beth didn't even know what his last name was, not that it mattered.

This morning, as usual, he went whistling along the walk to the Wilsons—he always stopped there first. Beth went to put out her ticket and found that she had none. She went for her purse, and taking out the money that she would need to purchase the tickets, she went to the back door. She waited for several minutes, and still Burt did not arrive. Surely he didn't miss me, she thought. He never has before.

She went back to the window and looked out at the back alley. No, his truck was still there. Beth stood at the window, waiting, glancing every now and then at the clock. The minutes ticked by slowly. Finally Burt appeared and walked to his truck while Beth stood wondering at her kitchen window.

The next morning it happened again. As Beth watched, she saw little Gary come running from the house just after Burt entered. She went out to shake her dust mop.

"Look what I've got," Gary said proudly, as he held up a chocolate bar. "He gave it to me."

The next morning Burt stopped again. This time, as he left the house, Marie was standing in the door. Beth gasped as she clearly saw Burt give Marie a little hug as he passed her to leave.

"I never would have believed it of her. She just didn't seem the type."

The days passed. Beth found herself waiting for the milk delivery each morning, and sure enough, each morning Burt stopped at the Wilsons. Beth noticed that he didn't stop to knock. One morning as she watched, she saw him walk directly in and over to Marie who was at her sink and give her a light kiss on the cheek.

"Something has got to be done. Her carrying on like that and then going to church and pretending that she's so—so—. Those poor little kids. Guess I'll just have to talk to Rev. Thomas."

Beth did have a talk with the pastor, but to her displeasure, he seemed very reluctant to take any action.

"I just can't understand it," Beth told Mildred. "He's supposed to be against sin, and there he sits with it right under his nose and won't do anything about it. The whole town knows that the Wilsons go to Faith, and when this gets out—and it will—people will think that we sanction this kind of action. Something just has to be done."

Beth repeated her story to the W.M.S. that met at her house on Thursday.

"We can't allow the church's name to be linked with such a thing. There has never been a scandal in the church before."

"You're sure . . . I mean . . . well, Mrs. Jamison seemed rather to think—"

"Mrs. Jamison doesn't think, you know that. Of course I'm sure. Would I be telling it if I weren't? One day he even bribed the little boy with a chocolate bar and sent him outside."

Beth snorted.

Mrs. Manville frowned.

"Oh my," she said. "Oh my," which was about as much as she ever ventured.

"Why," Beth looked at every woman in the ladies' group, "I've even seen them hugging and kissing—right in the open where anyone could see."

Even Mrs. Wright looked up at that. Beth noticed tears in her eyes.

"I was so sure that they'd find the Lord. So sure that soon . . . ." Her voice trailed off.

The following Sunday when the Wilsons arrived at church, they noticed an icy indifference on the part of some of the people. It was almost like being with strangers. Something was wrong, but they weren't sure what it was.

On Monday, Gary returned from the playground in tears.

"Randy says he can't play with me cause we're not good people. His Mommy says that we just pretend to be good when we go to church. Randy says I don't believe in Jesus. I do, don't I, Mommy?"

Marie finally got him quieted. So that was it. They were classed as sinners, and because of that, the church didn't want them. She decided to say nothing to Jim.

It was Judy who broke things wide open. At the Wednesday dinner table she said, with hurt in every word, "Candy Jamison said that she doesn't believe we're as bad as people at church say we are, and she wants to still be my friend anyway. What does she mean, Daddy?"

Jim looked up in surprise.

"Why, I don't know."

Then he added slowly, "Maybe they think that we should have 'confessed' by now. So that's why the cold shoulder and icy looks. Everywhere I go I can feel them looking at me. Well, if that's how they feel, they can have their church, and they can keep it pure—free from sinners. I won't ever enter . . . ."

"Jim, please," Marie stopped him. "Not in front of the children."

Judy carried the news to school the next day.

"We're not going to your church or Sunday School—not ever again."

When Rev. Thomas heard the news, he was much upset. Perhaps he'd better do a little looking into this. They had been such fine people and they needed the church and its message. Rev. Thomas decided to go to see Beth and find out more about what she had tried to tell him. Beth told him all and added, "I think that it would be terrible for folks to think that, just because they come to Faith, we don't condemn such actions."

"Well, I guess we won't need to worry about that," said Rev. Thomas, rising slowly. "They say that they aren't coming to Faith anymore."

Beth hesitated—but just for a moment.

"It's just as well. God will never bless us as long as there's sin in the camp. We can't expect Him to."

"But the Lord came to the lost—"

"Well, that certainly describes the Wilsons—though

I don't think that they know it. It would be different if they'd recognize their sin. But they pretend to be so goody-good and hide behind the church. We can't allow that. You know what had to be done to Achan!"

The pastor looked about to say something, then bit his lip and said that he must be getting back to his study.

Beth saw him to the door. So the Wilsons wouldn't be back. Maybe now the Lord could use the church.

Marie was in the yard when Burt arrived a couple of mornings later. They greeted one another and walked together to the house. As they entered the house, Burt placed his hand on her shoulder.

"Don't take it so hard," Beth heard him say.

The nerve—imagine the brazenness!

"Well, this has just gone far enough," Beth said to herself, jerking off her apron. "I'm just going to march over there and let them know that it's no secret."

Marie answered the door. She looked more than surprised, but managed a rather faltering smile as her composure returned.

"Well, she ought to be shook up," Beth thought.

"Won't you come into the kitchen for a cup of coffee?" Marie asked.

As she led the way, she continued. "Burt got his company's permission to take his morning coffee break here. Burt, this is my neighbor, Beth Robinson." Then, with a slight laugh, she added, "I guess you've known her for several years, but perhaps you haven't met officially. Beth, this is Burt—my brother."

I Wish I was a Turtle

Joseph Franklin Thomas lay on his stomach, head on his arms, on the banks of the Craemer Creek. The hot sun sent funny warm sensations through his body in the patches where it reached him through the leaves of the poplar branches. The smell of the earth made his nose twitch, and the waving grasses tickled his bare arms. Still, he did not move. He didn't feel like ever moving again. To him, life made no sense—no sense at all. Every time that it looked like something good was finally going to happen, something always went wrong. He'd been all fired up because today was the day for Little League try-outs. He'd hardly slept all night just thinking about them. For the last two years he'd been number two pitcher. Never quite good enough for number one—almost, but not quite—that was the story of his life. This year, with Gavin McConnell outgrowing the league, Joey was sure that he'd finally be in the number one spot.

He could hardly wait to get to the ball diamond. He'd done his paper route so fast that he arrived early, red-faced and panting. He was impatient for the action to begin—

for the coaches to get there with the equipment. This year he'd make it. He'd been Charlie Brown long enough—he felt that now it was the right time for him to break loose from his "bad luck."

Finally, things got under way and the team hopefuls got down to serious business. There were four trying out for pitchers—"Andy" Anderson, Jerry "Fats" Smiley, and a brand new boy by the name of Ralph. Andy and Jerry, Joey was not concerned about; he had seen what they could do many times, and he was sure that he had more on the ball than either of them. The new boy—that was something else—Joey felt his hackles rise, like a dog when a new dog enters his territory. Inwardly, he hoped with all of his heart that the new boy would be a bummer. He tried to act as though he couldn't care less when the new kid took a few warm-up pitches, but his heart was pounding. It was just as he had feared. This new Ralph kid was good. Joey wanted to smash him in the mouth; to convince the coaches that he couldn't last the game; to show him up by out-pitching him; to just run off by himself and cry. But he didn't do any of those things. He knew it was wrong to fight and even if he did get in a few punches, what good would that do? The coaches knew more than he did about pitchers and their strength, and they could see clearly that Ralph appeared to have staying-power. Joey went to the mound already feeling defeated and did what he could, but he knew that it just wouldn't be good enough to outpitch his opponent. He didn't cry—though with all of his being he wanted to—but he did die a little bit inside. There just was no sense to it, that was all.

As soon as he could get away, he had broken from the group and headed toward home. But when he had turned the corner out of sight from the ball park, he had wheeled his bike away from his familiar street and toward the creek.

He lay there now, sick feelings washing over him, flood after flood. He knew that he was already late for supper, and that meant more trouble. Mom and Dad would insist on knowing why he was late and where he had been. How could you say to your Mom and Dad that you just had to get off alone for awhile? They'd think it plumb silly for anyone to care that much about being number one on the team. They'd never understand. He could practically hear them—he'd heard it so often that it was like playing a recording.

"This is a recording . . . it's not important to be number one . . . the important thing is that you get to play the game and give it the best that you have . . . someone has to be number two, and remember that the other fellow wants to be number one just as much as you do . . . your coaches have to use the fellow who will most benefit the whole team . . . remember life is a series of disappointments . . . we have to learn to handle them like a man . . . that is maturity . . . the sooner you learn to handle your 'downs' the easier life will be on you . . . ."

Oh, he'd heard it all before—dozens of times. He doubted if ever a boy lived that had had more disappointments in life than he'd had. If "downs" made you a man as his dad said, he ought to be about the biggest man around. He'd had more than his rightful share.

It was like when someone said, "Pick a number between one and ten." If he said two, it'd be nine for sure; but if he said nine—.

And another thing, he reminded himself, the girls didn't like him either. He had thought that the cute new girl had been "going" to like him. She smiled at him a lot and seemed to giggle more when he came around. He had liked her, too, and really had hoped that maybe—but then he had chased her with a funny, squirmy bug just to tease her and to make her squeal. He was sure that she would understand about that—but she didn't—she told everybody that he was a creep and she never wanted to be anywhere near him again.

Fact was, he didn't really have any friends. Oh, some of the kids pretended to be his friends, especially when they got around the Dairy Queen and they knew that he had paper route money in his jeans pocket. They didn't really like him, he knew that now; nobody really cared what happened to him. His folks didn't know what it was even like to be a kid, with all of the hurts and pressures that one had to put up with. Soft—that's what grown-ups' world was.

No, his folks wouldn't understand. How could they? They'd never been through what he was going through. But he'd better get. He'd get chewed out for sure for being so late, maybe even have to miss the first game or something because of it. Well, he didn't care. They could make him miss all the games for all that he cared. He likely wouldn't get to play much anyway.

Even though he knew that he should have headed for home long ago, he lay still. The sun had moved on, warming different spots on his back than it had warmed at first. A black bug crawled across his arm and scurried into the grass. Joey watched it but didn't stir.

A small brown spotted turtle crawled up the creek bank toward him. Joey moved just enough to shove a stick across its path and the turtle stopped, pulling in its head in a quick movement. It stood for a few moments all bunched up in its shell; then, timidly, the head came out again, the eyes blinking, and the turtle started to move once more, picking a new route around the stick. Joey stuck the stick out again in the path. Again, the turtle retreated into its shell.

"Boy, have you got it made," said Joey. "Anything bothers you and you just up and bury yourself. Wish I could get away from everything and everybody that easy. Just pull in your head, pull in your legs. Hide from the whole world. Boy, have you got it easy."

The turtle didn't move. Joey poked it gently with the stick. It seemed to curl up even tighter.

"You're dumb, you know that?" Joey spoke to it. Don't you know that curling up in your shell don't solve nothing? I can still be here when you come out. Can wait all night if I want to. You ain't doing yourself no good at all just sitting there. You're dumb."

Joey watched as the turtle poked out its head again and then quickly jerked it back.

"Hiding away—that's what you're doing. Can't take it, can you? You're just plain dumb. Me, I gotta stay out and take everything that comes my way. I can't run off and hide like that. I gotta just take it 'on the chin' like Dad says. I gotta—"

Joey's voice trailed away. He had just seen something—very clearly for a boy of eleven.

"Yeah," he finally said. "I'm pretty dumb, too. Just dumb and stupid. I've been trying to crawl away and hide my head too just like you, Turtle—running down here and hiding in the grass instead of going home for supper. Laying here burying myself in 'feeling sorry's.' Guess I'm pretty dumb, too."

Joey got up and brushed the grass from his pants. He still felt all sad inside about the new kid and the pitching. He'd have to face Mom about being late for supper. Even worse, he'd have to face the guys tomorrow and hear them rave about that new kid and all of the games he'd be sure to win for them. Life could be pretty tough at times—sometimes it hardly seemed worth the effort—but it didn't seem to help much to try to crawl away.

He climbed aboard his bike and headed for home. The sun was getting low in the sky. Boy, he really was late.

Mom sure would be upset. Joey bet that the new guy had already had his supper and bragged to his folks about his great pitching and what the coaches said and all.

"Well, why should I . . ." began Joey to himself, then did an abrupt shift of thought. "Hey . . . wonder, if I take him for a chocolate malt, if he'd help me work on my curve ball . . . . ?"

No Strings Attached

Viney brushed a wispy bit of hair back from her forehead.

"I must be a mess," she thought. "My hair feels like it's standing on end."

No wonder, the way it had been tossed and ruffled to try to free it from some of its load of confetti.

"What a day," she sighed. "What a wonderful day."

Yes, it had all been glorious. But now, as it neared its end, she suddenly realized just how tired she was.

"Ron must be tired too," she thought. "Poor Ron."

They had just pulled into their honeymoon cabin when he had discovered a flat tire. All of the service stations would be closed tomorrow, so it would have to be fixed tonight.

"You look tired," he had said. "I'll take in the luggage and you use these few minutes to rest and freshen up. I'll be right back and then we'll go out for a snack."

It sounded like a good idea to Viney. She pushed her foot free of her shoe.

"Whew, feels like I bought them three sizes too small," she chided herself, then stretched out across the bed.

Her mind went back over the day, the ceremony, then back still farther to their courtship.

"Oh, I'm so lucky. So very lucky."

Suddenly she felt uneasy as she recalled the words of Norma, her maid of honor.

"Well, Viney, looks like you've got it made—if you don't have mother-in-law problems."

Mother-in-law problems! Viney had never considered it before. Mrs. Mayland—Mother Mayland, she corrected herself—had always been very sweet and very wise, too, in Viney's eyes.

Seeing the look in Viney's eyes, Norma hurried on.

"Oh, don't get me wrong. I think she's fine. But—well—really, you know what I mean. Ron has been her pride and joy for twenty-six years. You don't expect her to forget that overnight, do you? I mean—well—she is a widow you know, and everyone knows that the two of them are as close as that." She crossed two fingers. "Really, Viney—oh, skip it."

She kissed Viney's cheek lightly.

"Happiness to you both."

Just before Ron and Viney departed for their honeymoon, Mother Mayland had kissed Viney fondly on the cheek and then pressed a rather bulky, sealed envelope into her hand.

"Open it later," she whispered.

Norma's eyes opened wide and as Mother Mayland passed on to kiss Ron farewell, Norma leaned to Viney and whispered.

"Prob'ly full of instructions on how to care for her darling boy. You know: be sure he gets a good breakfast, never bother him before his cup of coffee, make sure he wears his raincoat, etc."

She made a face.

Now, remembering the envelope, Viney reached for her handbag. Her hand almost trembled as she pulled out the small package. She fingered it for a moment, fearful that its contents might somehow change her feelings for her new mother-in-law. Then, almost hurriedly, she tore it open and let the contents tumble onto the bed beside her.

For a moment she stared, trying hard to figure out the meaning of the strange little parcel. Then her eyes filled with tears, and a smile flickered across her face.

"Dear Mother Mayland," she whispered, as she lovingly picked up the carefully pressed and folded pieces of material. She recognized them at once as the ties from Mother Mayland's favorite apron.

Mother's Apron Strings

There are chains of iron unyielding,
Enduring under stress and strain.
There are ropes of steel-like texture
Bound together grain on grain.

But there's not a pull or binding
More secure though ages roll,
Though all manner of times testing
Tries in vain to take its toll,

Than the simple, frail it seemeth,
Yet in weakness, a strong thing,
For it holds a world upon it—
Mother's humble apron string.

Yes, they're simple, oh so simple,
Tied into a knot with care;
But no common, mere onlooker
Sees the hearts all tied up there.

Through the days of early childhood,
When the Mother, young in years,
Watched with love the tiny toddler,
Saw the falls, the hurts, the tears,

Wiped the tears upon her apron,
Placed the feet upon the floor,
And with look of understanding,
Urged him try it out once more.

There were days when he was naughty,
Needed lessons hard to learn.
Mother heard of "child-psychology,"
But its methods she did spurn.

For she had her own convictions.
In correction she was gifted.
So, across her checkered apron,
She her naughty child lifted.

Then the days of childhood problems,
Troubled looks in questioning eyes,
Caused her to turn for a moment
From half-ready crusts for pies,

Wipe her hands upon her apron,
Draw the wee one to her side,
And discuss the "urgent" problem
Till the child was satisfied.

Teenage followed early childhood.
Problems seemed to multiply.
Teenage "words of wisdom" often
Brought the tear to Mother's eye.

There were times of deep rebellion
  When many unkind words were said.
Though at times he was unyielding,
  It hurt when Mother turned her head

And her hand reached for her apron.
  Then he knew he wasn't fair,
Also knew that in her silence
  It was tears that she wiped there.

Though he had the power to hurt her,
  She would only pray the more;
And her love would never waver,
  Though her heart was sad and sore.

Mother was much like her apron,
  Uncomplaining, roughly used,
Giving silently in service,
  Feeling not she was abused.

Only later do we realize
  All her love has had to bear,
And our own love swells within us.
  "Bless her, Father," is our prayer.

"May she realize we love her,
  All her prayers were not in vain.
May her guiding and instructing
  Now bear fruit in golden grain."

Only now we fully realize
  Each seed has been sown with prayer;
Each hard lesson had its purpose,
  And it left impressions there.

And the things we thought important,
  Are, perhaps, just little things.
And little things take on new meaning . . .
  Such as Mother's apron strings.

They Just Have Everything

The breezes sighed contentedly among the tall aspens, and the smell of blossoms filled the night air. Don breathed deeply. He loved the evening, especially when it meant he could be with Vicki.

Vicki—with her soft brown curls and deep blue eyes, the long misty eyelashes falling on fair cheeks, smiling lips and soft dimple—this was Vicki.

He loved Vicki more than he had thought it possible for a man to love a girl. His future was filled with plans for her. Each activity, each thought that he had, was built around her. She was the drive behind his attainment, his real reason for success. His wife was going to have the best that money could buy.

Don had always had his share of "things," but for Vicki it had been different. At one time she had lived in a fine, though not elaborate, home. Then tragedy had struck—leaving her a homeless orphan, determined to fend for herself.

It had been a bright spring day, the woods dripping

with moisture and the brooks pushing and tumbling in their haste to get to the river which was already overflowing its banks, when a sudden roar was heard. For miles around, the deep rumble sounded, growing in volume. Those within range of the sound realized, with a feeling of great panic, that the Glenview Dam had broken.

Vicki's parents' farm was in a verdant valley, right in the path that the wall of water must take. With little time for planning, Vicki's father ran to the nearby pasture where the saddle horse was grazing. Hurriedly boosting the two girls onto the pony's back, he gave them a quick hug and told them to ride hard, straight up the hillside. He and their mother would follow.

The girls did as they had been told, urging the horse in its wild flight up the hill. When they reached the safety of the hillside, they turned to see how far behind them their parents were; but only raging flood waters stretched beneath them and roared on down the valley. It was too late.

The neighbors in the valley were kind to the orphan girls. As soon as they had finished high school, both of the girls went to work to support themselves.

It was at a church picnic that Don had first met Vicki. She was dressed in a cream-colored pant suit. The ruffled blouse of blue matched her eyes—eyes which laughed and teased, in spite of the past's haunting memories.

Vicki was busy in an ice cream booth, and Don figured that he must have eaten more ice cream that day than anyone else there—although he noticed, with concern, that several fellows his age were also frequent visitors at the booth.

From then on he saw a lot of Vicki, and the better he knew her the more deeply he loved her. It was that way with Vicki too. The very way that she looked at him assured him that she loved him. She paid no attention at all to the many boys who tried to get her attention.

When Jean, Vicki's older sister, had married Bob Dutton, Vicki was even more alone in the world. Jean tried to pursuade Vicki to move in with them, but Vicki declined, knowing that they deserved to have their new life together without intruders—even if it be a kid sister. Vicki did visit Bob and Jean frequently. It was after a visit to Bob and Jean's, to help them celebrate their first anniversary, that Don had asked Vicki to marry him. He remembered how her eyes shone with love as she looked up at him. His heart fairly sang.

At first they had planned to be married the next spring. Then Don had done some calculating and decided that he would not have saved enough by then to give Vicki the things that he wanted her to have. He was even more sure of the decision when, on a date one night, Vicki told him with sparkling eyes that Bob and Jean "just had everything." Poor kid! She had forgotten what it was to have "everything." Bob and Jean only had a small, two-bedroom house that seemed even smaller since Tommy had arrived. Still, they were happy. Well, maybe some folks were content with so little, but Don wanted his wife to be able to show her home with pride.

Vicki had seemed disappointed when he asked her if she minded waiting another year. But she agreed that he knew best. Now the year was nearly up, and Don had seen the house that he wanted Vicki to have. He had saved much toward the house—but not enough for the down payment, plus the furnishings that it would need. He had also planned a honeymoon in Bermuda, though he had not told Vicki.

Don dreaded it, but he had decided that tonight he would ask Vicki to postpone the wedding for another year. She might rebel at first—he could picture the disappointment in the flashing eyes—but she'd come around.

He was sure of that. She was a reasonable person and she trusted his judgment.

He quickened his step as he turned up the walk to Bob and Jean's house. Vicki had promised Jean that she would babysit with small Tommy, and Don had been invited to join her there.

As usual, he was aware of a quickening of his pulse at the thought of seeing her. He pushed the doorbell and waited.

A moment later the door swung open. A slender girl, dressed in blue jeans and a sweater, held it open with one hand. The teasing eyes gazed steadily into his, and her free hand took his and eased him in.

"Oh, it's just you. I thought it was George."

Why did she always have to tease him? She was forever catching him off-guard with one thing or another. He could just imagine the mischief shining in her eyes when she was a kid.

Immediately her eyes softened and only love shone there. The door swung closed behind him and he took her into his arms. Her arms circled his neck as their lips met with tender eagerness.

She was the first to pull back from the embrace.

"I thought you'd never come," she smiled. "Tommy has been asleep for hours."

It was a wonderful evening. They played records, worked a crossword puzzle together, snacked, and just sat and talked. Suddenly Don looked at his watch. Vicki noticed it.

"What's the matter?" she teased, "Afraid you'll miss your beauty sleep or afraid to walk home after midnight?"

She reached over and with a caressing hand ruffled his dark wavy hair.

He smiled at her.

"Time has just flown, hasn't it?"

Inwardly he said to himself, "I'd better get it over with. They'll soon be home. Anyway she's in such a wonderful mood tonight she won't mind at all."

"Vick."

He was the only one who ever said her name that way, and each time that he did it made her heart skip a beat. All of his love seemed to be transferred into that one syllable.

She turned to look at him.

"Vick, I've been thinking. Don't you think it might be wise to wait another year to be married?"

She looked at him in blank amazement. Then her eyelids fell and he saw tears ease out from beneath them. Slowly she rose to her feet and moved to the window.

He did not speak for he did not know what to say. He just watched the graceful form standing alone against the dark outline of the black outdoors, held back only by a pane of glass. Somehow he felt cut off from Vicki—like the darkness was cut off from the bright, cheery room.

His heart pleaded with her to understand. It was for her that he was doing it.

There was a sigh and the slim shoulders seemed to droop. Vicki began to turn. Without meaning to, Don sighed also. His sigh was one of relief; Vicki's had been one of resignation.

Instead of sitting down beside him again, Vicki crossed to the big easy chair. Letting her shoes slide noiselessly onto the rug, she tucked her feet up beneath her. She looked like a bewildered little girl. She still did not look up.

"Why don't we wait two years, Don, or maybe three?"

Her voice sounded weary—alone. There was not the sparkle there that usually accompanied Vicki's speaking.

"Two years? Three? But Vicki, one is bad enough. I'm not waiting two years."

He stood up suddenly to show his concern.

"What makes you want to wait two years—or three?"

She still did not raise her eyes.

"I didn't say that I wanted to wait three, or two either. I just thought that I'd save you the trouble of lengthening it another year next year at this time."

"Vicki—"

"You know that you will, don't you, Don? I don't think you want to get married. I think that you're just stalling. If you don't want to, just say so—don't—"

She raised her eyes to his as he stood before her. Once again the tears ran down her cheeks. She looked so tiny, so alone. Don would have given anything to take her in his arms and kiss the tears away; still he dared not try. She seemed locked away from him—beyond his reach. Her eyes held his.

"You don't have to marry me, you know. Don, if you're not ready to settle down . . . ."

She stopped. Once again her gaze fell to the floor, and again the tears made an appearance.

"But I am ready to get married," Don protested. "Honest, Vicki, I want to marry you more than anything else that I've ever wanted."

She sniffed.

"Really?"

"Of course."

He knelt before her and lifted her hand in his. The light fell across the ring on her left hand and sent drops of rainbow around the room. It was their ring—his and Vicki's.

At the sound of a silvery laugh, his head jerked up and he looked again into two teasing deep blue eyes.

"Then maybe it's me. Maybe I'm the one who has to grow up. Maybe you're waiting on me. Perhaps I should have had my fling and then I'd be ready to settle down."

She pulled her hand from his and stared at the ring.

"Do you suppose I should go call George?"

She didn't even know a George and he knew it. Again her eyes twinkled like those of a taunting child. He stood up helplessly. She looked up at him and laughed. The tears on her cheeks seemed a faded memory now, as though she had already forgotten that she had shed them and now they were deserted—deserted like she herself had seemed to feel a few short moments ago.

He believed, as he looked at her, that she had even forgotten that she had been given reason to cry. Why the sudden change? Had she decided that she wasn't ready for marriage after all? What had he done?

A moment before she had been as a broken-hearted child—lonely, hurt, and confused—and he had longed to take her into his arms and comfort her. Then suddenly she had turned into a strange, teasing creature, with sparkling eyes and taunting lips, laughing in the very face of love. If he had wanted to take her in his arms before, now he yearned to, doubly so.

Suddenly the quiet was shattered by the cry of a baby.

Her eyes filled with tender concern as she untucked her feet from beneath her and hurried to Tommy's room. By the time she reached the baby, he was crying loudly, as though frightened.

Don listened as the baby's cries softened into quiet sobs and then stopped entirely. He stole quietly to the door of the room.

Vicki stood with the baby held close to her. She said nothing, but her eyes spoke volumes as she gazed tenderly at the small boy in her arms. Don had never seen her eyes so tender. Her face was radiant. He recalled Vicki's words, "They just have everything," and suddenly he understood.

He took a step inside the door and Vicki looked up. She had not seen him standing there.

Her eyes seemed to apologize for her quick retreat.

"He's sleeping now," she whispered. "He must have had a bad dream."

She turned and gently laid the sleeping baby in his crib. Don noted the tenderness with which she tucked him in.

She straightened and again her eyes were filled with pain and disappointment, as though another year to wait for a home of her own was almost asking too much. This time Don understood.

"Vick?"

She waited.

"Vick. How soon could you be ready to be married?"

She blinked, as though she had not understood.

"Look, Hon," his words seemed to run over one another in their rush to be said. "There's a little house over on Beech Street . . . it's not much but it could be fixed up real cute . . . and if we just took a short honeymoon trip, we'd be able to furnish it and could fix it to move into right away."

He stopped for breath. She still just stared at him. What had he done now? Was she going to ask him to leave and go look up someone by the name of George? Vicki, please say something, his heart pleaded.

"Oh, Don."

With a glad rush, Vicki was in his arms, her tear-stained face buried against him. A moment later, a shining face, still wet with tears, turned to meet his.

"You're so wonderful," she whispered.

He didn't say anything; what could he say? He just held her closer. Oh well, he never would understand women, at least not Vicki—his Vicki.

He wondered anew at the beauty of the sweep of the downturned lashes on the soft fair cheeks, then bent to kiss the teasing lips.

A Lesson from Sandra

A true life experience of the author.

Restlessly, I moved my head back and forth on the pillow, conscious only of the ache in my throat—the ache that I could not swallow away. In my semi-consciousness I tried fighting off sleep, feeling sure that when I fully awakened I would find the pain only part of a dream. Then a rustle in the room made me realize that it had been activity rather than pain that had aroused me. Yes, the pain was still there, real and aching. But I most certainly would have slept on, regardless of it, had not the quiet yet disturbing presence of "someone" been heard and felt.

I turned my head toward the movement. Very quietly, a white-clad nurse was helping a young lady as she settled into bed. A new bed, too, had been added to the room—a small basket into which a tiny baby girl was carefully placed. As I watched, I wondered what circumstances brought the new occupants to the hospital room. Was it the young mother or the tiny baby who needed the doctor's care? Since entering the small town hospital the night before and having a tonsilectomy that morning, I had been alone in the room. Having been told by my doctor that I must remain for a few days for shots to clear my system of infection, I found it comforting to know that I would have company. Being in my very early teens, I did not in the least look forward to days of aloneness. Still, I felt curiosity and pity for the room's new guests. Poor young mother. It must be serious for her to have to come in the middle of the night this way. Soon my senses were accustomed to the new sounds and light, and because drugs still demanded that I sleep, I turned over and was again in the world of dreams.

When morning came I was to learn much about my new roommates. The young mother, Mrs. McLeod, had made a long and hurried trip to get her two-week-old baby Sandra to the doctors. She spoke with a trembling voice when she told of the experience. The baby was having serious difficulty in breathing because of mucus that would gather in the throat. Once on the way they were sure they would be too late, but they were able to clear her throat sufficiently for her to breathe again.

I fell in love with little Sandra immediately. She looked like the picture an expectant mother would, with hope in her heart, pin on her bedroom wall. It was hard for me to believe that there were other little ones at home. I had thought Mrs. McLeod too young to have older children, but she spoke lovingly of them and of the excitement they had felt when the new baby came home, and of their fear and disappointment when their mother and baby sister had to hurriedly leave for the hospital. Mrs. McLeod was alone now, many miles from the home where her husband and she farmed in a rather sparsely populated area. Her husband had returned home almost immediately to be with the little ones, and the trip was too distant to make for visiting hours. Because of her aloneness she talked to me —a young gangly kid with wide eyes and an open heart— and partly because of the soreness of my throat, but mostly because of the shyness that I had always felt, I listened quietly. While I listened, my heart filled with prayer that little Sandra would be all right and my mind filled with pity for Mrs. McLeod. I thought, too, of the little children at home, waiting anxiously for the return of their mother and the little sister that they had already learned to love. Then my mind went back a few years to one of the most happy and unforgettable experiences of my young life.

The whole house was in a commotion. But perhaps the most excitement was felt by Margie, my sister two years my junior, and me; for soon Mama would leave to get the promised new baby. What could be more wonderful? I could still see my Mother letting us gently place our hands upon her and feel the movement of the baby. Now, she explained, the time was soon to be, for the baby was knocking, "Let me out," so it could be with the rest of the family. Yes, it was a sad time to see Mama drive away, but the promise of what her return would bring brought brave smiles to our faces. Besides, Grandma was there to look after us, so we would make out—we would do it for the new baby. At long, long last we heard the good news—we had a new baby sister. Just think of it. A real baby sister of our very own. The next big thrill was in naming her. Margie picked Ruth after a girl who had worked for my mother, and I liked Joyce because of one of my Sunday School friends. Other members of the family also gave their suggestions, but the new baby was named Joyce Ruth. We had named her and that made her even more ours. The long days dragged by, but at last the day came when Mother brought the new baby home. Oh, she was tiny—one could scarcely see her in the blankets. When I took her tiny hand she even kind of smiled, I thought. She even had hair. I was glad for that. I had seen one baby that didn't have—not even a little bit. When she finally got around to opening her eyes, they were blue, real blue.

Even when we went to play the excitement stayed with us. Our new baby was home. She was ours and we were going to be able to watch her grow, and she'd like us for big sisters because we'd be real good to her. The days passed and the new baby brought joy each day. I remembered one event with clarity. I came in from my play and there in the big farm kitchen Mama was bathing our baby. The oven door was open to give added warmth to the room. I watched as the bath was finished. I really hadn't realized before how soft and pudgy she was. Her little arms and legs waved excitedly. They were all dimples and cuddlyness, and then my Mother looked at me and smiled.

"Would you like to hold her before I dress her?"

I was too thrilled to speak but my eyes must have said it for me, for she summoned me to stand before the oven door for a moment to make sure that I wasn't cold. Then, after a check of my hands and clothes, she placed the wriggling baby sister in my arms. I giggled in excitement, and even though Mother's hand also supported the baby, I mentally disregarded that and for the moment felt like the most privileged person in the world, for I was holding my little sister—naked and squirming and all my own.

My thoughts were interrupted and I was again in the hospital room with a worried young mother who would give anything to take her baby home to her little family. The troubled eyes of the mother and the heavy breathing of the baby reminded me of the seriousness of the situation. Would those little ones at home be denied all of the joys that I had found in my baby sister? Would this young mother be forced to return to her family heart-broken and alone? And precious little Sandra—what of her? I choked up at the thought of it. A soft footstep of the nurse announced "needle time" again. With relief I saw my favorite nurse enter, bearing a tray with the needed equipment. She was always so gentle, in both voice and touch, that the needle was not to be so dreaded when she administered it. A word of encouragement, a pat on the arm, or a smile went with her from bed to bed. Here was a real nurse, I thought. But perhaps the secret lay in the fact that she too had known the stab of pain and the long hours of suffering. As she picked up the tray, and smiling said, "I wish all of my patients would take a needle like that," I forgot the momentary sting in my hip. I watched as she turned and left the room. Her walk gave her secret away. She too had been a victim of the much dreaded polio but had unselfishly returned to a life of service to others.

The afternoon brought added concern, for little Sandra had another bad spell, and after suctioning her throat of its life-endangering fluid, she was placed in an incubator for easier breathing. As there was no nurse available to stay with her and she was the only baby in the small room, Mrs. McLeod went to keep watch. She did not wish to sit alone, so with the nurse's permission, I went to the nursery to be company in her vigil. As we watched the sleeping baby, we talked—of many things, none of them really important, and yet they succeeded in occupying our minds and filling our minutes. Suddenly, our eyes became more intent upon the baby as the gasps for air became quicker and more frantic. Then slowly the little body began to turn a bluish shade. Mrs. McLeod cried frantically, "I'm going for the nurse. You stay here," and ran from the room. I stayed, completely helpless. Was I to simply stand there and watch baby Sandra die? Yet there was nothing I could do. Then running steps told me that help was near and my favorite nurse hurried into the room. She threw back the glass lid and with the suction pump began to work on the baby. Then she took the little legs and began slowly, accurately, coaxing life back into the little body.

I stumbled out of the small room and down the hall to my own, to find Mrs. McLeod thrown across her bed in hysterical tears. I, too, was crying as I crossed to her bed. There was only one hope.

"Have you tried prayer?" I sobbed, in a voice mumbled by tears.

"That's all I've been doing," she answered.

"I'll pray, too." The words were hardly audible because of my accompanying sobs. I found my way to my bed and in tears and pleas asked God to undertake on behalf of little Sandra.

It seemed an eternity—but in actuality was only a short time—until we heard the familiar step in the hall. Would the bearer bring good tidings, or would the news be crushing? Neither of us dared look at her face as she entered, but the soft voice held a note of victory.

"Mrs. McLeod, your baby is going to be all right." Mrs. McLeod threw herself across her pillow as a fresh burst of tears overcame her, and in uncontrollable thankfulness, she cried, "Oh, thank God."

Little Sandra did get better. By the time I left the hospital she was well on her way to recovery. The little family waiting at home would be able to enjoy their baby because of the goodness of God. We both realized that He was the One who had given the little life and He also had been kind enough to restore it. We knew, too, that our own visions had been enlarged. A young Catholic mother and a gangly Protestant kid had shared a burden, lifted prayer together, and Heaven had moved in response. There was a strange bond between us, one that only such sharing brings. After all, God the Father was *our* Father. Did not Scripture say in John 1:12, "But as many as received Him, to them gave He the power to become the sons of God"?

Discard

Gran Adamson sat, pen in hand, pondering just what to say in her letter to her missionary son, Jim. She had written him only brief notes that were very general in scope the last two times, but she knew that she wouldn't be able to put Jim off with that for long. He would be wanting to know how things were "really" going, and Gran finally felt up to getting to work on "that" letter.

Still, it was hard just knowing where to start. She sat thinking back over the past few months of her life.

She knew that the year had been a very difficult one for Norma, her oldest daughter and their only child near at hand. Norma had always been such a serious person, even as a very small child. Gran, as "mother," had often wished that she could take the sober girl and get her to act less grown-up and more like a carefree child. But that was Ruthie. Ruthie never had a thought for anything. Life was a game to her. She couldn't take anything seriously. If only the two girls could have equalized their two extremes, but there didn't seem to be any way that she, as a parent, could do that for them.

Norma had grown up a good girl, even though a serious one. She had been awfully good to Dad and Gran, even though she worried too much.

Ruthie had grown up, too—at least to some degree—though they had often wondered if she would ever grow up at all. When she did leave home, Gran felt lost without her happy, easy-going, bustling little self around. There was no one to remind to "pick up your jacket, put away the peanut butter, stop clowning, hang up the hand-towel, practice your music, stop clowning."

But that was all so long ago. Jim had been with the Mission for almost thirty years and before they knew it, would be due to retire. She couldn't feature Jim retired. They'd have to find something for him to do. His children were grown and on their own as well. Ruthie had grown and married a boy who seemed willing enough to put up with her lack of seriousness. In fact, Cal seemed to prefer her that way—that was the way they lived—a little scatter-brained perhaps— changing jobs with changing moods, Dad used to say. She guessed that Norma had inherited her seriousness from her father. He never would have considered anything so foolish as changing jobs just so that you could get a look at another part of the country. Now Ruthie and Cal and their three teen-agers were living in Georgia, because Ruthie always felt that it sounded like such a "romantic" place. Gran smiled, wondering if her head-in-the-clouds daughter had found it "romantic" with its hot weather and bugs. That was Gran's feeling about any place south of the Canadian border.

With Jim in Kenya, and Ruthie flitting here and there, wherever the globe beckoned, the sole responsibility of caring for Mom and Dad fell on the shoulders of their steady old Norma. Even though Norma might lack a sense of humor, she had been more than good in her thoughtfulness for her parents. Gran remembered the many times that Norma had appeared when they needed her; her eyes filled with sincere concern. Birthdays—it was Norma who brought over the cake and made the day a bright one for them. Christmas—it was Norma who picked them up and drove them to her house to get in on the "family" Christmas. In sickness—it was Norma who was there, making sure that the doctor was called and that the medicine he left was taken as directed. Sundays—it was Norma who drove almost three miles out of her way to make sure that they had a ride to church. Yes, Norma had been a dear daughter, and every day Gran thanked God for giving her to them.

It was while Norma was busy with the preparations for Tanya's wedding that things began to change. Tanya—it had always been a mystery to Gran why a practical soul like Norma would name her first daughter Tanya. In fact, she had chosen catchy little names for all three of her children. She had named her boy Keaton. It wasn't such a bad name, though it had taken some getting used to, not like the names of Bill or Jim like the family usually stayed with. The youngest, another girl, Norma had named Yolinda Jo. Even quiet Dad made a comment on that one. Mind you, he did say it under his breath, but still Gran had distinctly heard him, as he looked down on the tiny bundle, say, "Poor little thing," very softly.

Gran reminded herself that her mind was wandering again. She had been trying to recall the events surrounding Tanya's wedding.

Norma had been rushed nearly off her feet, trying to have everything "just so" for her eldest daughter's wedding. There were days that she was so busy that she didn't even make a phone call, which was very unlike Norma. However, she came whenever she could squeeze a few minutes into her busy schedule and did the shopping for them and looked after anything that they couldn't care for themselves.

Gran admitted that "Dad" had failed in the last two years or so. She had to yell to make herself heard at times, and he didn't read as much as he used to. Oh, he still sat in his chair with a magazine or book, but usually he slept while the book lay unread in his lap. He wandered around some, too, as though looking for something, but never sure just what it was. This bothered Norma. It was hard for a person to see her parents grow old, Gran knew. But, land's sake, Norma was a grandma herself now; surely she must realize that they grew older along with her.

Anyway, Norma was busy and didn't get over the last few days before the wedding. And, about that time, Gran happened to pick up a "bug" of some kind. It did rather get her down. She fussed with mustard plasters and Vicks, but it didn't seem to shake it much. When Norma came in the day before the wedding to see what they might be in need of and to set the time for picking them up for the wedding, she nearly had a fit. "Why didn't you call?" she kept saying, as though they were completely unable to do anything for themselves. She hastened to call the doctor, who promptly came over and ordered Gran to the hospital, so that she missed her granddaughter's wedding. Gran felt it a little difficult to forgive the doc for that. He could have given her a shot or something and let her stay on her feet.

Well, that had sort of got things rolling. When Gran did finally get back home, it took a long while to seem to get her strength back. She didn't say anything about it, but she guessed it showed; for Norma, and even her husband Ted, started making remarks about her unsteadiness. It wasn't that she was still weak, it was just that she didn't seem to be able to get her silly feet under her where they were supposed to be. It seemed that everytime she got up to head for something, her feet seemed to want to go another way, or get there faster or slower than the rest of her—or something. Anyway, after Norma noticed it, Gran could feel her eyes on her, watching her every move. She couldn't even get up for the teapot without Norma getting all set to jump to steady her. It unnerved her a bit. She even got so that she sat stubbornly at times and let Norma get up for more tea.

That's when Norma started making comments about the lovely facilities at the Royal Oak Manor. Gran fairly snorted. Royal Oak Manor—fiddlesticks! It was just a fancy name for an old folk's home, that's what it was. Why didn't they call it what it really was instead of trying to make one think that they were on a long holiday in some fancy hotel or some such.

Well, Norma really convinced herself that they should be where they could be watched by a doctor, fed proper meals, and generally cared for. They resisted—they were doing just fine. True, Dad sometimes forgot to take his pill, but he usually made it up in the next day or two—forgetting that he had already taken it and so taking another. It sort of evened itself out, Gran figured, but Norma didn't see it that way. Then Gran had taken a rather nasty fall. It happened one morning at breakfast. Dad liked brown sugar on his porridge. Gran hadn't made porridge. She was feeling a little "off her feed," so she had put some cold cereal on the table for their breakfast. She had already sat down when she remembered that she had forgotten the brown sugar. She hurried up to get it and had taken about two steps when she noticed that her feet weren't keeping up to the rest of her. She went down rather hard, smacking her forehead on the door frame. It had cut it some—not enough to worry about—but Dad got a little upset and couldn't find even a Band-Aid to fix it up. So he called Norma. She was over in next to no time. By then Gran had washed her forehead with a damp cloth and got it covered with some bandage and adhesive, and was washing up the dishes. Even that hadn't convinced Norma.

"Mother," she said in that very serious voice, "please give it some serious thought."

"That's what you're for," Gran wanted to answer. "You're the one with the serious thoughts." But Gran didn't say it. She knew that Norma really was worried about them. She knew, too, that Norma had been doing a lot of praying about the matter and felt strongly that the Royal Oak Manor was the answer to her prayers. Well, maybe Norma was right. It was getting a bit hard to keep up to the work of the house. Whenever Norma came over she cleaned out the fridge, wrinkling her nose at food that smelled perfectly good to Gran, or she fussed over clothes that Gran could see no wrinkles in, or scrubbed in corners that Gran hadn't noticed to be dirty. Well, maybe the work was getting a little hard to keep up with. Dad was a bit of a problem at times, Gran conceded, but she had always been able to humor him along.

Finally, Gran decided to have a talk with Dad about it. Funny, thought Gran, he had stayed "Dad," while she had long since become "Gran" to all who knew her.

She had her talk with Dad. He didn't seem to care too much one way or the other. His only comment had been, "Norma knows best. If that's what Norma thinks, then that's what we should do."

It irritated Gran a bit that Dad had put them in the league of no longer being able to make a rational decision. She knew that Norma would be relieved. She phoned her and told her to go ahead and make the arrangements.

Things had happened so fast that Gran had a suspicion that Norma must have had the ball already rolling before she got her call. Oh, well, now that she had made up her mind, she was rather anxious to get it all over with.

They wouldn't be allowed to take much with them in the line of personal things. Dad was granted his rather worn chair that fit him in all the right places. Gran decided on a set of shelves. At least she still wanted her family's pictures with her. Somehow things were arranged for, and the day for the move arrived. They were up early as usual, not being used to sleeping in in the mornings. After breakfast they packed up their suitcases and prepared to wait for Norma.

Gran decided to add a little humor to the event and took an old piece of corn flakes box and wrote across it in big letters, with an old red crayon, "DISCARD," and pinned it on the front of her dress. Dad looked at it and mumbled that she was being a little silly, but she left it there anyway, thinking that it might give Norma a good laugh. She should have known better. Norma came in already looking like she had spent the morning in tears, and when she saw the sign, she said, "Oh, Mama"—just like that—and burst forth crying.

"What you need is a sense of humor, girl," Gran said as she took off the sign and threw it in the wastepaper basket. She felt bad. She hadn't meant to make Norma feel bad. The last few months had been very hard on her she knew, and Norma was doing what she felt was the only thing to do. Norma had been so good, looking out for them all these years and bearing the full burden of their care. She crossed to Norma and put her arm around her, to assure her that she really did feel okay about going to the home. She was determined that she was going to refer to it as it really was, not by some fancy name.

Norma finally got herself in hand, and they set off for what was to be their new residence. Somehow, Gran couldn't think of it as "home."

Gran stopped to stare again at the blank paper that was to have been her letter to Jim.

They had been here for two weeks now. Dad was restless at first. Now he spent so much time down chawing with some of the other old-timers that his chair hardly got any use. He seemed to have a little more spunk now that his medicine was taken regularly. Yes, she guessed that maybe the move had been good for Dad.

She was getting rather used to it herself. She had never admitted it, not even to herself, but she had grown terribly tired of fixing meals day after day. It was rather nice to be welcomed to a table, anticipating a "surprise" meal. Then there was the matter of the laundry. All that Gran had to do now was to put out her laundry bag for collection, and the clothes were returned the next day all washed and pressed. She didn't even have to be concerned about Dad's medication. A smiling lady appeared at the table each morning, giving out the medications needed.

She had worried at first about having time on her hands and that she would be just sitting there in a corner of her room waiting for another day to tick slowly by. She had been surprised at the number of things to get involved in. There was a crafts club, a Bible study group, vesper services, games and T.V., and even an exercise club. The ladies often got together in small groups to play a game of Scrabble, or to put together a jig-saw puzzle, or just to brag a bit about their families and share experiences of life. No, it really wasn't so bad.

Gran looked out of the window and noticed that there was light snow falling. It looked pretty as it floated softly down. How wild the kids used to get over the year's first snowfall. She felt relief, though, that she wouldn't have to worry about Dad trying to take care of the shoveling of the walk himself. She used to pray until he was safely indoors again, afraid that he would have a heart attack or slip on the frozen walk. Well, she wouldn't have to worry about that this year. She was glad.

She looked back at the still empty sheet before her, but her mind wouldn't stay with it. The snow made her think that it wouldn't be too long until Christmas would be coming. Just yesterday, her Bible study group had talked about putting on their own little Christmas program for the rest of the residents in the manor. They had gotten all enthusiastic about it and had begun to plan what they would do. Gran was to play the piano for the carol sing. She hadn't played much in the last few years and was anxious to do some practicing.

She brought her mind back to the letter that she was to write. In a rather wobbly and slow hand she wrote across the top right side, "Royal Oak Manor"—it did sound rather impressive. She had a bit of a problem figuring out the date. Yesterday was Bible Club; on the tenth of the month was to be a film of New Zealand, and they hadn't had that yet. Norma had phoned this morning saying, "I'll see you tomorrow." It was Keaton's twenty-second birthday (Keaton was away to college and wouldn't be home). Gran remembered that Keaton was born on November ninth at three fifteen in the afternoon. It had been a stormy day with the temperature well below zero, and Ted had been scared half to death that the car wouldn't start. But it had, and Norma had been safely admitted before Keaton had made his appearance. Tomorrow would be Keaton's birthday, so today must be November eighth. Gran added that to her letter.

She looked up then at the little clock that ticked quietly on her shelf. "My word," she exclaimed. It was already ten past two. The girls would be waiting. It was craft club time, and she was going to show them the right way to do a new crochet stitch that some of them were having trouble with. They were making cushion tops. She was going to give hers to Norma for Christmas. Well, her letter would just have to wait, decided Gran. She jumped up to get her things together, then remembered the nurse's instructions and took a few minutes to steady herself on her feet before heading for the craft room.